Charlotte Mary Yonge

A Modern Telemachus

Outlook

Charlotte Mary Yonge

A Modern Telemachus

1. Auflage | ISBN: 978-3-73261-928-3

Erscheinungsort: Paderborn, Deutschland

Erscheinungsjahr: 2018

Outlook Verlag GmbH, Paderborn.

A MODERN TELEMACHUS

'Be still; I want to hear what they are saying.'—P. 2.

ILLUSTRATED BY W. J. HENNESSY.

London
MACMILLAN AND CO.
AND NEW YORK
1889

All rights reserved

First Edition (2 *Vols. Crown* 8*vo*) 1886
Reprinted 1887, 1889

1

PREFACE

The idea of this tale was taken from *The Mariners' Chronicle*, compiled by a person named Scott early in the last century—a curious book of narratives of maritime adventures, with exceedingly quaint illustrations. Nothing has ever shown me more plainly that truth is stranger than fiction, for all that is most improbable here is the actual fact.

The Comte de Bourke was really an Irish Jacobite, naturalised in France, and married to the daughter of the Marquis de Varennes, as well as in high favour with the Marshal Duke of Berwick.

In 1719, just when the ambition of Elizabeth Farnese, the second wife of Philip V. of Spain, had involved that country in a war with England, France, and Austria, the Count was transferred from the Spanish Embassy to that of Sweden, and sent for his wife and two elder children to join him at a Spanish port.

This arrangement was so strange that I can only account for it by supposing that as this was the date of a feeble Spanish attempt on behalf of the Jacobites in Scotland, Comte de Bourke may not have ventured by the direct route. Or it may not have been etiquette for him to re-enter France when appointed ambassador. At any rate, the poor Countess did take this route to the South, and I am inclined to think the narrative must be correct, as all the side-lights I have been able to gain perfectly agree with it, often in an unexpected manner.

The suite and the baggage were just as related in the story—the only liberty I have taken being the bestowal of names. 'M. Arture' was really of the party, but I have made him Scotch instead of Irish, and I have no knowledge that the lackey was not French. The imbecility of the Abbé is merely a deduction from his helplessness, but of course this may have been caused by illness.

The meeting with M. de Varennes at Avignon, Berwick's offer of an escort, and the Countess's dread of the Pyrenees, are all facts, as well as her embarkation in the Genoese tartane bound for Barcelona, and its capture by the Algerine corsair commanded by a Dutch renegade, who treated her well, and to whom she gave her watch.

Algerine history confirms what is said of his treatment. Louis XIV. had bombarded the pirate city, and compelled the Dey to receive a consul and to liberate French prisoners and French property; but the lady having been taken in an Italian ship, the Dutchman was afraid to set her ashore without first

2

taking her to Algiers, lest he should fall under suspicion. He would not venture on taking so many women on board his own vessel, being evidently afraid of his crew of more than two hundred Turks and Moors, but sent seven men on board the prize and took it in tow.

Curiously enough, history mentions the very tempest which drove the tartane apart from her captor, for it also shattered the French transports and interfered with Berwick's Spanish campaign.

The circumstances of the wreck have been closely followed. 'M. Arture' actually saved Mademoiselle de Bourke, and placed her in the arms of the *maître d'hôtel*, who had reached a rock, together with the Abbé, the lackey, and one out of the four maids. The other three were all in the cabin with their mistress and her son, and shared their fate.

The real 'Arture' tried to swim to the shore, but never was seen again, so that his adventures with the little boy are wholly imaginary. But the little girl's conduct is perfectly true. When in the steward's arms she declared that the savages might take her life, but never should make her deny her faith.

The account of these captors was a great difficulty, till in the old *Universal History* I found a description of Algeria which tallied wonderfully with the narrative. It was taken from a survey of the coast made a few years later by English officials.

The tribe inhabiting Mounts Araz and Couco, and bordering on Djigheli Bay, were really wild Arabs, claiming high descent, but very loose Mohammedans, and savage in their habits. Their name of Cabeleyzes is said—with what truth I know not—to mean 'revolted,' and they held themselves independent of the Dey. They were in the habit of murdering or enslaving all shipwrecked travellers, except subjects of Algiers, whom they released with nothing but their lives.

All this perfectly explains the sufferings of Mademoiselle de Bourke. The history of the plundering, the threats, the savage treatment of the corpses, the wild dogs, the councils of the tribe, the separation of the captives, and the child's heroism, is all literally true—the expedient of Victorine's defence alone being an invention. It is also true that the little girl and the *maître d'hôtel* wrote four letters, and sent them by different chances to Algiers, but only the last ever arrived, and it created a great sensation.

M. Dessault is a real personage, and the kindness of the Dey and of the Moors was exactly as related, also the expedient of sending the Marabout of Bugia to negotiate.

Mr. Thomas Thompson was really the English Consul at the time, but his share in the matter is imaginary, as it depends on Arthur's adventures.

The account of the Marabout system comes from the *Universal History*; but the arrival, the negotiations, and the desire of the sheyk to detain the young French lady for a wife to his son, are from the narrative. He really did claim to be an equal match for her, were she daughter of the King of France, since he was King of the Mountains.

The welcome at Algiers and the *Te Deum* in the Consul's chapel also are related in the book that serves me for authority. It adds that Mademoiselle de Bourke finally married a Marquis de B–, and lived much respected in Provence, dying shortly before the Revolution.

I will only mention further that a rescued Abyssinian slave named Fareek (happily not tongueless) was well known to me many years ago in the household of the late Warden Barter of Winchester College.

Since writing the above I have by the kindness of friends been enabled to discover Mr. Scott's authority, namely, a book entitled *Voyage pour la Redemption des captifs aux Royaumes d'Alger et de Tunis, fait en* 1720 *par les P.P. François Comelin, Philemon de la Motte, et Joseph Bernard, de l'Ordre de la Sainte Trinité, dit Mathurine*. This Order was established by Jean Matha for the ransom and rescue of prisoners in the hands of the Moors. A translation of the adventures of the Comtesse de Bourke and her daughter was published in the *Catholic World*, New York, July 1881. It exactly agrees with the narration in *The Mariners' Chronicle* except that, in the true spirit of the eighteenth century, Mr. Scott thought fit to suppress that these ecclesiastics were at Algiers at the time of the arrival of Mademoiselle de Bourke's letter, that they interested themselves actively on her behalf, and that they wrote the narrative from the lips of the *maître d'hôtel* (who indeed may clearly be traced throughout). It seems also that the gold cups were chalices, and that a complete set of altar equipments fell a prey to the Cabeleyzes, whose name the good fathers endeavour to connect with *Cabale*—with about as much reason as if we endeavoured to derive that word from the ministry of Charles II.

Had I known in time of the assistance of these benevolent brethren I would certainly have introduced them with all due honour, but, like the Abbé Vertot, I have to say, *Mon histoire est écrite*, and what is worse—printed. Moreover, they do not seem to have gone on the mission with the Marabout from Bugia, so that their presence really only accounts for the *Te Deum* with which the redeemed captives were welcomed.

It does not seem quite certain whether M. Dessault was Consul or Envoy; I incline to think the latter. The translation in the *Catholic World* speaks of Sir

Arthur, but Mr. Scott's 'M. Arture' is much more *vraisemblable*. He probably had either a surname to be concealed or else unpronounceable to French lips. Scott must have had some further information of the after history of Mademoiselle de Bourke since he mentions her marriage, which could hardly have taken place when Père Comelin's book was published in 1720.

C. M. YONGE.

CHAPTER I—COMPANIONS OF THE VOYAGE

'Make mention thereto
Touching my much loved father's safe return,
If of his whereabouts I may best hear.'

Odyssey (MUSGRAVE).

'Oh! brother, I wish they had named you Télémaque, and then it would have been all right!'

'Why so, sister? Why should I be called by so ugly a name? I like Ulysses much better; and it is also the name of my papa.'

'That is the very thing. His name is Ulysses, and we are going to seek for him.'

'Oh! I hope that cruel old Mentor is not coming to tumble us down over a great rook, like Télémaque in the picture.'

'You mean Père le Brun?'

'Yes; you know he always says he is our Mentor. And I wish he would change into a goddess with a helmet and a shield, with an ugly face, and go off in a cloud. Do you think he will, Estelle?'

'Do not be so silly, Ulick; there are no goddesses now.'

'I heard M. de la Mêde tell that pretty lady with the diamond butterfly that she was his goddess; so there are!'

'You do not understand, brother. That was only flattery and compliment. Goddesses were only in the Greek mythology, and were all over long ago!'

'But are we really going to see our papa?'

'Oh yes, mamma told me so. He is made Ambassador to Sweden, you know.'

'Is that greater than Envoy to Spain?'

'Very, very much greater. They call mamma Madame l'Ambassadrice; and she is having three complete new dresses made. See, there are *la bonne* and Laurent talking. It is English, and if we go near with our cups and balls we shall hear all about it. Laurent always knows, because my uncle tells him.'

'You must call him *La Juenesse* now he is made mamma's lackey. Is he not beautiful in his new livery?'

'Be still now, brother; I want to hear what they are saying.'

This may sound somewhat sly, but French children, before Rousseau had made them the fashion, were kept in the background, and were reduced to picking up intelligence as best they could without any sense of its being dishonourable to do so; and, indeed, it was more neglect than desire of concealment that left their uninformed.

This was in 1719, four years after the accession of Louis XV., a puny infant, to the French throne, and in the midst of the Regency of the Duke of Orleans. The scene was a broad walk in the Tuileries gardens, beneath a closely-clipped wall of greenery, along which were disposed alternately busts upon pedestals, and stone vases of flowers, while beyond lay formal beds of flowers, the gravel walks between radiating from a fountain, at present quiescent, for it was only ten o'clock in the forenoon, and the gardens were chiefly frequented at that hour by children and their attendants, who, like Estelle and Ulysse de Bourke, were taking an early walk on their way home from mass.

They were a miniature lady and gentleman of the period in costume, with the single exception that, in consideration of their being only nine and seven years old, their hair was free from powder. Estelle's light, almost flaxen locks were brushed back from her forehead, and tied behind with a rose-coloured ribbon, but uncovered, except by a tiny lace cap on the crown of her head; Ulick's darker hair was carefully arranged in great curls on his back and shoulders, as like a full-bottomed wig as nature would permit, and over it he wore a little cocked hat edged with gold lace. He had a rich laced cravat, a double-breasted waistcoat of pale blue satin, and breeches to match, a brown velvet coat with blue embroidery on the pockets, collar, and skirts, silk stockings to match, as well as the knot of the tiny scabbard of the semblance of a sword at his side, shoes with silver buckles, and altogether he might have been a full-grown Comte or Vicomte seen through a diminishing glass. His sister was in a full-hooped dress, with tight long waist, and sleeves reaching to her elbows, the under skirt a pale pink, the upper a deeper rose colour; but stiff as was the attire, she had managed to give it a slight general air of disarrangement, to get her cap a little on one side, a stray curl loose on her forehead, to tear a bit of the dangling lace on her arms, and to splash her robe with a puddle. He was in air, feature, and complexion a perfect little dark Frenchman. The contour of her face, still more its rosy glow, were more in accordance with her surname, and so especially were the large deep blue eyes with the long dark lashes and pencilled brows. And there was a lively restless air about her full of intelligence, as she manoeuvred her brother towards a stone seat, guarded by a couple of cupids reining in sleepy-looking lions in stone, where, under the shade of a lime-tree, her little petticoated brother of two years old was asleep, cradled in the lap of a large, portly, handsome woman, in a dark dress, a white cap and apron, and dark crimson cloak, loosely put back, as it was an August day. Native costumes were then, as now, always worn by French nurses; but this was not the garb of any province of the kingdom, and was as Irish as the brogue in which she was conversing with the tall fine young man who stood at ease beside her. He was in a magnificent green and gold livery suit, his hair powdered, and fastened in a *queue*, the whiteness contrasting with the dark brows, and the eyes and complexion of that fine Irish type that it is the fashion to call Milesian. He looked proud of his dress, which was viewed in those days as eminently becoming, and did in fact display his well-made figure and limbs to great advantage; but he looked anxiously about, and his first inquiry on coming on the scene in attendance upon the little boy had been—

'The top of the morning to ye, mother! And where is Victorine?'

'Arrah, and what would ye want with Victorine?' demanded the *bonne*. 'Is not the old mother enough for one while, to feast her eyes on her an' Lanty Callaghan, now he has shed the *marmiton's* slough, and come out in old Ireland's colours, like a butterfly from a palmer? La Jeunesse, instead of Laurent here, and Laurent there.'

La Pierre and La Jeunesse were the stereotyped names of all pairs of lackeys in French noble houses, and the title was a mark of promotion; but Lanty winced and said, 'Have done with that, mother. You know that never the pot nor the kettle has blacked my fingers since Master Phelim went to the good fathers' school with me to carry his books and insinse him with the larning. 'Tis all one, as his own body-servant that I have been, as was fitting for his own foster-brother, till now, when not one of the servants, barring myself and Maître Hébert, the steward, will follow Madame la Comtesse beyond the four walls of Paris. "Will you desert us too, Laurent?" says the lady. "And is it me you mane, Madame," says I, "Sorrah a Callaghan ever deserted a Burke!" "Then," says she, "if you will go with us to Sweden, you shall have two lackey's suits, and a couple of *louis d'or* to cross your pocket with by the year, forbye the fee and bounty of all the visitors to M. le Comte." "Is it M. l'Abbé goes with Madame?" says I. "And why not," says she. "Then," says I, "'tis myself that is mightily obliged to your ladyship, and am ready to put on her colours and do all in reason in her service, so as I am free to attend to Master Phelim, that is M. l'Abbé, whenever he needs me, that am in duty bound as his own foster-brother." "Ah, Laurent," says she, "'tis you that are the faithful domestic. We shall all stand in need of such good offices as we can do to one another, for we shall have a long and troublesome, if not dangerous journey, both before and after we have met M. le Comte.'''

Estelle here nodded her head with a certain satisfaction, while the nurse replied—

'And what other answer could the son of your father make—Heavens be his bed—that was shot through the head by the masther's side in the weary wars in Spain? and whom could ye be bound to serve barring Master Phelim, that's lain in the same cradle with yees—'

'Is not Victorine here, mother?' still restlessly demanded Lanty.

'Never you heed Victorine,' replied she. 'Sure she may have a little arrand of her own, and ye might have a word for the old mother that never parted with you before.'

'You not going, mother!' he exclaimed.

''Tis my heart that will go with you and Masther Phelim, my jewel; but Madame la Comtesse will have it that this weeny little darlint'—caressing the child in her lap—'could never bear the cold of that bare and dissolute place in the north you are bound for, and old Madame la Marquise, her mother, would be mad entirely if all the children left her; but our own lady can't quit the little one without leaving his own nurse Honor with him!'

'That's news to me intirely, mother,' said Lanty; 'bad luck to it!'

Honor laughed that half-proud, half-sad laugh of mothers when their sons outgrow them. 'Fine talking! Much he cares for the old mother if he can see the young girl go with him.'

For Lanty's eyes had brightened at sight of a slight little figure, trim to the last degree, with a jaunty little cap on her dark hair, gay trimmings to the black apron, dainty shoes and stockings that came tripping down the path. His tongue instantly changed to French from what he called English, as in pathetic insinuating modulations he demanded how she could be making him weary his very heart out.

'Who bade you?' she retorted. 'I never asked you to waste your time here!'

'And will ye not give me a glance of the eyes that have made a cinder of my poor heart, when I am going away into the desolate north, among the bears and the savages and the heretics?'

'There will be plenty of eyes there to look at your fine green and gold, for the sake of the Paris cut; though a great lumbering fellow like you does not know how to show it off!'

'And if I bring back a heretic *bru* to break the heart of the mother, will it not

10

be all the fault of the cruelty of Mademoiselle Victorine?'

Here Estelle, unable to withstand Lanty's piteous intonations, broke in, 'Never mind, Laurent, Victorine goes with us. She went to be measured for a new pair of slices on purpose!'

'Ah! I thought I should disembarrass myself of a great troublesome Irishman!'

'No!' retorted the boy, 'you knew Laurent was going, for Maître Hébert had just come in to say he must have a lackey's suit!'

'Yes,' said Estelle, 'that was when you took me in your arms and kissed me, and said you would follow Madame la Comtesse to the end of the world.'

The old nurse laughed heartily, but Victorine cried out, 'Does Mademoiselle think I am going to follow naughty little girls who invent follies? It is still free to me to change my mind. Poor Simon Claquette is gnawing his heart out, and he is to be left *concierge*!'

The clock at the palace chimed eleven, Estelle took her brother's hand, Honor rose with little Jacques in her arms, Victorine paced beside her, and Lanty as La Jeunesse followed, puffing out his breast, and wielding his cane, as they all went home to *déjeuner*.

Twenty-nine years before the opening of this narrative, just after the battle of Boyne Water had ruined the hopes of the Stewarts in Ireland, Sir Ulick Burke had attended James II. in his flight from Waterford; and his wife had followed him, attended by her two faithful servants, Patrick Callaghan, and his wife Honor, carrying her mistress's child on her bosom, and her own on her back.

Sir Ulick, or Le Chevalier Bourke, as the French called him, had no scruple in taking service in the armies of Louis XIV. Callaghan followed him everywhere, while Honor remained a devoted attendant on her lady, doubly bound to her by exile and sorrow.

Little Ulick Burke's foster-sister died, perhaps because she had always been made second to him through all the hardships and exposure of the journey. Other babes of both lady and nurse had succumbed to the mortality which beset the children of that generation, and the only survivors besides the eldest Burke and one daughter were the two youngest of each mother, and they had arrived so nearly at the same time that Honor Callaghan could again be foster-mother to Phelim Burke, a sickly child, reared with great difficulty.

The family were becoming almost French. Sir Ulick was an intimate friend of one of the noblest men of the day, James Fitz-James, Marshal Duke of Berwick, who united military talent, almost equal to that of his uncle of

Marlborough, to an unswerving honour and integrity very rare in those evil times. Under him, Sir Ulick fought in the campaigns that finally established the House of Bourbon upon the throne of Spain, and the younger Ulick or Ulysse, as his name had been classicalised and Frenchified, was making his first campaign as a mere boy at the time of the battle of Almanza, that solitary British defeat, for which our national consolation is that the French were commanded by an Englishman, the Duke of Berwick, and the English by a Frenchman, the Huguenot Rubigné, Earl of Galway. The first English charge was, however, fatal to the Chevalier Bourke, who fell mortally wounded, and in the endeavour to carry him off the field the faithful Callaghan likewise fell. Sir Ulick lived long enough to be visited by the Duke, and to commend his children to his friend's protection.

Berwick was held to be dry and stiff, but he was a faithful friend, and well redeemed his promise. The eldest son, young as he was, obtained as wife the daughter of the Marquis de Varennes, and soon distinguished himself both in war and policy, so as to receive the title of Comte de Bourke.

The French Church was called on to provide for the other two children. The daughter, Alice, became a nun in one of the Parisian convents, with promises of promotion. The younger son, Phelim, was weakly in health, and of intellect feeble, if not deficient, and was almost dependent on the devoted care and tenderness of his foster-brother, Laurence Callaghan. Nobody was startled when Berwick's interest procured for the dull boy of ten years old the Abbey of St. Eudoce in Champagne. To be sure the responsibilities were not great, for the Abbey had been burnt down a century and a half ago by the Huguenots, and there had never been any monks in it since, so the only effect was that little Phelim Burke went by the imposing title of Monsieur l'Abbé de St. Eudoce, and his family enjoyed as much of the revenues of the estates of the Abbey as the Intendant thought proper to transmit to them. He was, to a certain degree, ecclesiastically educated, having just memory enough to retain for recitation the tasks that Lanty helped him to learn, and he could copy the themes or translations made for him by his faithful companion. Neither boy had the least notion of unfairness or deception in this arrangement: it was only the natural service of the one to the other, and if it were perceived in the Fathers of the Seminary, whither Lanty daily conducted the young Abbot, they winked at it. Nor, though the quick-witted Lanty thus acquired a considerable amount of learning, no idea occurred to him of availing himself of it for his own advantage. It sat outside him, as it were, for 'Masther Phelim's' use; and he no more thought of applying it to his own elevation than he did of wearing the *soutane* he brushed for his young master.

The Abbé was now five-and-twenty, had received the tonsure, and had been admitted to minor Orders, but there was no necessity for him to proceed any farther unless higher promotion should be accorded to him in recompense of his brother's services. He was a gentle, amiable being, not at all fit to take care of himself; and since the death of his mother, he had been the charge of his brother and sister-in-law, or perhaps more correctly speaking, of the Dowager Marquise de Varennes, for all the branches of the family lived together in the Hotel de Varennes at Paris, or its chateau in the country, and the fine old lady ruled over all, her son and son-in-law being often absent, as was the case at present.

A fresh European war had been provoked by the ambition of the second wife of Philip V. of Spain, the Prince for whose cause Berwick had fought. This Queen, Elizabeth Farnese, wanted rank and dominion for her own son; moreover, Philip looked with longing eyes at his native kingdom of France, all claim to which he had resigned when Spain was bequeathed to him; but now that only a sickly child, Louis XV., stood between him and the succession in right of blood, he felt his rights superior to those of the Duke of Orleans. Thus Spain was induced to become hostile to France, and to commence the war known as that of the Quadruple Alliance.

While there was still hope of accommodation, the Comte de Bourke had been sent as a special envoy to Madrid, and there continued even after the war had broken out, and the Duke of Berwick, resigning all the estates he had received from the gratitude of Philip V., had led an army across the frontier.

The Count had, however, just been appointed Ambassador to Sweden, and was anxious to be joined by his family on the way thither.

The tidings had created great commotion. Madame de Varennes looked on Sweden as an Ultima Thule of frost and snow, but knew that a lady's presence was essential to the display required of an ambassador. She strove, however, to have the children left with her; but her daughter declared that she could not part with Estelle, who was already a companion and friend, and that Ulysse must be with his father, who longed for his eldest son, so that only little Jacques, a delicate child, was to be left to console his grandmother.

CHAPTER II—A JACOBITE WAIF

'Sac now he's o'er the floods sae gray,
And Lord Maxwell has ta'en his good-night.'

LORD MAXWELL'S *Good-night.*

Madame La Comtesse de Bourke was by no means a helpless fine lady. She had several times accompanied her husband on his expeditions, and had only not gone with him to Madrid because he did not expect to be long absent, and she sorely rued the separation.

She was very busy in her own room, superintending the packing, and assisting in it, when her own clever fingers were more effective than those of her maids. She was in her *robe de chambre*, a dark blue wrapper, embroidered with white, and put on more neatly than was always the case with French ladies in *déshabille*. The hoop, long stiff stays, rich brocade robe, and fabric of powdered hair were equally unsuitable to ease or exertion, and consequently were seldom assumed till late in the day, when the toilette was often made in public.

So Madame de Bourke's hair was simply rolled out of her way, and she appeared in her true colours, as a little brisk, bonny woman, with no actual beauty, but very expressive light gray eyes, furnished with intensely long black lashes, and a sweet, mobile, lively countenance.

Estelle was trying to amuse little Jacques, and prevent him from trotting between the boxes, putting all sorts of undesirable goods into them; and Ulysse had collected his toys, and was pleading earnestly that a headless wooden horse and a kite, twice as tall as himself, of Lanty's manufacture, might go with them.

He was told that another *cerf-volant* should be made for him at the journey's end; but was only partially consoled, and his mother was fain to compound for a box of woolly lambs. Estelle winked away a tear when her doll was rejected, a wooden, highly painted lady, bedizened in brocade, and so dear to her soul that it was hard to be told that she was too old for such toys, and that the Swedes would be shocked to see the Ambassador's daughter embracing a doll. She had, however, to preserve her character of a reasonable child, and tried to derive consolation from the permission to bestow 'Mademoiselle' upon the *concierge's* little sick daughter, who would be sure to cherish her duly.

'But, oh mamma, I pray you to let me take my book!'

'Assuredly, my child. Let us see! What? Télémaque? Not "Prince Percinet and Princess Gracieuse?"'

'I am tired of them, mamma.'

'Nor Madame d'Aulnoy's Fairy Tales?'

'Oh no, thank you, mamma; I love nothing so well as Télémaque.'

'Thou art a droll child!' said her mother.

'Ah, but we are going to be like Télémaque.'

'Heaven forfend!' said the poor lady.

'Yes, dear mamma, I am glad you are going with us instead of staying at home to weave and unweave webs. If Penelope had been like you, she would have gone!'

'Take care, is not Jacques acting Penelope?' said Madame de Bourke, unable to help smiling at her little daughter's glib mythology, while going to the rescue of the embroidery silks, in which her youngest son was entangling himself.

At that moment there was a knock at the door, and a message was brought that the Countess of Nithsdale begged the favour of a few minutes' conversation in private with Madame. The Scottish title fared better on the lips of La Jeunesse than it would have done on those of his predecessor. There was considerable intimacy among all the Jacobite exiles in and about Paris; and Winifred, Countess of Nithsdale, though living a very quiet and secluded life, was held in high estimation among all who recollected the act of wifely heroism by which she had rescued her husband from the block.

Madame de Bourke bade the maids carry off the little Jacques, and Ulysse followed; but Estelle, who had often listened with rapt attention to the story of the escape, and longed to feast her eyes on the heroine, remained in her corner, usefully employed in disentangling the embroilment of silks, and with the illustrations to her beloved Télémaque as a resource in case the conversation should be tedious. Children who have hundreds of picture-books to rustle through can little guess how their predecessors could once dream over one.

Estelle made her low reverence unnoticed, and watched with eager eyes as the slight figure entered, clad in the stately costume that was regarded as proper respect to her hostess; but the long loose sacque of blue silk was faded, the *feuille-morte* velvet petticoat frayed, the lace on the neck and sleeves washed and mended; there were no jewels on the sleeves, though the long gloves fitted exquisitely, no gems in the buckles of the high-heeled shoes, and the only ornament in the carefully rolled and powdered hair, a white rose. Her face was thin and worn, with pleasant brown eyes. Estelle could not think her as beautiful as Calypso inconsolable for Ulysses, or Antiope receiving the boar's a head. 'I know she is better than either,' thought the little maid; 'but I wish she was more like Minerva.'

The Countesses met with the lowest of curtseys, and apologies on the one side for intrusion, on the other for *déshabille*, so they concluded with an embrace really affectionate, though consideration for powder made it necessarily somewhat theatrical in appearance.

These were the stiffest of days, just before formality had become unbearable, and the reaction of simplicity had set in; and Estelle had undone two desperate knots in the green and yellow silks before the preliminary compliments were over, and Lady Nithsdale arrived at the point.

'Madame is about to rejoin *Monsieur son Mari*.'

'I am about to have that happiness.'

'That is the reason I have been bold enough to derange her.'

'Do not mention it. It is always a delight to see *Madame la Comtesse*.'

'Ah! what will Madame say when she hears that it is to ask a great favour of her.'

'Madame may reckon on me for whatever she would command.'

'If you can grant it—oh! Madame,' cried the Scottish Countess, beginning to drop her formality in her eagerness, 'we shall be for ever beholden to you, and you will make a wounded heart to sing, besides perhaps saving a noble young spirit.'

'Madame makes me impatient to hear what she would have of me,' said the French Countess, becoming a little on her guard, as the wife of a diplomatist, recollecting, too, that peace with George I. might mean war with the Jacobites.

'I know not whether a young kinsman of my Lord's has ever been presented to Madame. His name is Arthur Maxwell Hope; but we call him usually by his Christian name.'

'A tall, dark, handsome youth, almost like a Spaniard, or a picture by Vandyke? It seems to me that I have seen him with M. le Comte.' (Madame de Bourke could not venture on such a word as Nithsdale.)

'Madame is right. The mother of the boy is a Maxwell, a cousin not far removed from my Lord, but he could not hinder her from being given in marriage as second wife to Sir David Hope, already an old man. He was good to her, but when he died, the sons by the first wife were harsh and unkind to her and to her son, of whom they had always been jealous. The eldest was a creature of my Lord Stair, and altogether a Whig; indeed, he now holds an office at the Court of the Elector of Hanover, and has been created one of *his* peers. (The scorn with which the gentle Winifred uttered those words was worth seeing, and the other noble lady gave a little derisive laugh.) 'These half-brothers declared that Lady Hope was nurturing the young Arthur in Toryism and disaffection, and they made it a plea for separating him from her, and sending him to an old minister, who kept a school, and who was very severe and even cruel to the poor boy. But I am wearying Madame.'

'Oh no, I listen with the deepest interest.'

'Finally, when the King was expected in Scotland, and men's minds were full of anger and bitterness, as well as hope and spirit, the boy—he was then only fourteen years of age—boasted of his grandfather's having fought at Killiecrankie, and used language which the tutor pronounced treasonable. He was punished and confined to his room; but in the night he made his escape and joined the royal army. My husband was grieved to see him, told him he had no right to political opinions, and tried to send him home in time to make his peace before all was lost. Alas! no. The little fellow did, indeed, pass out safely from Preston, but only to join my Lord Mar. He was among the gentlemen who embarked at Banff; and when my Lord, by Heaven's mercy, had escaped from the Tower of London, and we arrived at Paris, almost the first person we saw was little Arthur, whom we thought to have been safe at home. We have kept him with us, and I contrived to let his mother know that he is living, for she had mourned him as among the slain.'

'Poor mother.'

'You may well pity her, Madame. She writes to me that if Arthur had returned at once from Preston, as my Lord advised, all would have been passed over as a schoolboy frolic; and, indeed, he has never been attainted; but there is nothing that his eldest brother, Lord Burnside as they call him, dreads so much as that it should be known that one of his family was engaged in the campaign, or that he is keeping such ill company as we are. Therefore, at her request, we have never called him Hope, but let him go by our name of Maxwell, which is his by baptism; and now she tells me that if he could make his way to Scotland, not as if coming from Paris or Bar-le-Duc, but merely as if travelling on the Continent, his brother would consent to his return.'

'Would she be willing that he should live under the usurper?'

'Madame, to tell you the truth,' said Lady Nithsdale, 'the Lady Hope is not one to heed the question of usurpers, so long as her son is safe and a good lad. Nay, for my part, we all lived peaceably and happily enough under Queen Anne; and by all I hear, so they still do at home under the Elector of Hanover.'

'The Regent has acknowledged him,' put in the French lady.

'Well,' said the poor exile, 'I know my Lord felt that it was his duty to obey the summons of his lawful sovereign, and that, as he said when he took up arms, one can only do one's duty and take the consequences; but oh! when I look at the misery and desolation that has come of it, when I think of the wives not so happy as I am, when I see my dear Lord wearing out his life in banishment, and think of our dear home and our poor people, I am tempted to wonder whether it were indeed a duty, or whether there were any right to call on brave men without a more steadfast purpose not to abandon them!'

'It would have been very different if the Duke of Berwick had led the way,' observed Madame de Bourke. 'Then my husband would have gone, but, being French subjects, honour stayed both him and the Duke as long as the Regent made no move.' The good lady, of course, thought that the Marshal Duke and her own Count must secure victory; but Lady Nithsdale was intent on her own branch of the subject, and did not pursue 'what might have been.'

'After all,' she said, 'poor Arthur, at fourteen, could have no true political convictions. He merely fled because he was harshly treated, heard his grandfather branded as a traitor, and had an enthusiasm for my husband, who had been kind to him. It was a mere boy's escapade, and if he had returned home when my Lord bade him, it would only have been remembered as such. He knows it now, and I frankly tell you, Madame, that what he has seen of our exiled court has not increased his ardour in the cause.'

'Alas, no,' said Madame de Bourke. 'If the Chevalier de St. George were other than he is, it would be easier to act in his behalf.'

'And you agree with me, Madame,' continued the visitor, 'that nothing can be worse or more hopeless for a youth than the life to which we are constrained here, with our whole shadow of hope in intrigue; and for our men, no occupation worthy of their sex. We women are not so ill off, with our children and domestic affairs; but it breaks my heart to see brave gentlemen's lives thus wasted. We have done our best for Arthur. He has studied with one of our good clergy, and my Lord himself has taught him to fence; but we cannot treat him any longer as a boy, and I know not what is to be his future, unless we can return him to his own country.'

'Our army,' suggested Madame de Bourke.

'Ah! but he is Protestant.'

'A heretic!' exclaimed the lady, drawing herself up. 'But—'

'Oh, do not refuse me on that account. He is a good lad, and has lived enough among Catholics to keep his opinions in the background. But you understand that it is another reason for wishing to convey him, if not to Scotland, to some land like Sweden or Prussia, where his faith would not be a bar to his promotion.'

'What is it you would have me do?' said Madame de Bourke, more coldly.

'If Madame would permit him to be included in her passport, as about to join the Ambassador's suite, and thus conduct him to Sweden; Lady Hope would find means to communicate with him from thence, the poor young man would be saved from a ruined career, and the heart of the widow and mother would bless you for ever.

Madame de Bourke was touched, but she was a prudent woman, and paused to ask whether the youth had shown any tendency to run into temptation, from which Lady Nithsdale wished to remove him.

'Oh no,' she answered; 'he was a perfectly good docile lad, though high-spirited, submissive to the Earl, and a kind playfellow to her little girls; it was his very excellence that made it so unfortunate that he should thus be stranded in early youth in consequence of one boyish folly.'

The Countess began to yield. She thought he might go as secretary to her Lord, and she owned that if he was a brave young man, he would be an addition to her little escort, which only numbered two men besides her brother-in-law, the Abbé, who was of almost as little account as his young nephew. 'But I should warn you, Madame,' added Madame de Bourke, 'that it may be a very dangerous journey. I own to you, though I would not tell my poor mother, that my heart fails me when I think of it, and were it not for the express commands of their father, I would not risk my poor children on it.'

'I do not think you will find Sweden otherwise than a cheerful and pleasant abode,' said Lady Nithsdale.

'Ah! if we were only in Sweden, or with my husband, all would be well!' replied the other lady; 'but we have to pass through the mountains, and the Catalans are always ill-affected to us French.'

'Nay; but you are a party of women, and belong to an ambassador!' was the answer.

'What do those robbers care for that? We are all the better prey for them! I have heard histories of Spanish cruelty and lawlessness that would make you shudder! You cannot guess at the dreadful presentiments that have haunted me ever since I had my husband's letter.'

'There is danger everywhere, dear friend,' said Lady Nithsdale kindly; 'but God finds a way for us through all.'

'Ah! you have experienced it,' said Madame de Bourke. 'Let us proceed to the affairs. I only thought I should tell you the truth.'

Lady Nithsdale answered for the courage of her *protégé*, and it was further determined that he should be presented to her that evening by the Earl, at the farewell reception which Madame de Varennes was to hold on her daughter's behalf, when it could be determined in what capacity he should be named in the passport.

Estelle, who had been listening with all her ears, and trying to find a character in Fénelon's romance to be represented by Arthur Hope, now further heard it explained that the party were to go southward to meet her father at one of the Mediterranean ports, as the English Government were so suspicious of Jacobites that he did not venture on taking the direct route by sea, but meant to travel through Germany. Madame de Bourke expected to meet her brother at Avignon, and to obtain his advice as to her further route.

Estelle heard this with great satisfaction. 'We shall go to the Mediterranean Sea and be in danger,' she said to herself, unfolding the map at the beginning of her Télémaque; 'that is quite right! Perhaps we shall see Calypso's island.'

She begged hard to be allowed to sit up that evening to see the hero of the escape from the Tower of London, as well as the travelling companion destined for her, and she prevailed, for mamma pronounced that she had been very sage and reasonable all day, and the grandmamma, who was so soon to part with her, could refuse her nothing. So she was full dressed, with hair curled, and permitted to stand by the tall high-backed chair where the old lady sat to receive her visitors.

The Marquise de Varennes was a small withered woman, with keen eyes, and a sort of sparkle of manner, and power of setting people at ease, that made her the more charming the older she grew. An experienced eye could detect that she retained the costume of the prime of Louis XIV., when headdresses were less high than that which her daughter was obliged to wear. For the two last mortal hours of that busy day had poor Madame de Bourke been compelled to sit under the hands of the hairdresser, who was building up, with paste and powder and the like, an original conception of his, namely, a northern landscape, with snow-laden trees, drifts of snow, diamond icicles, and even a cottage beside an ice-bound stream. She could ill spare the time, and longed to be excused; but the artist had begged so hard to be allowed to carry out his brilliant and unique idea, this last time of attending on Madame l'Ambassadrice, that there was no resisting him, and perhaps her strange forebodings made her less willing to inflict a disappointment on the poor man. It would have been strange to contrast the fabric of vanity building up outside her head, with the melancholy bodings within it, as she sat motionless under the hairdresser's fingers; but at the end she roused herself to smile gratefully, and give the admiration that was felt to be due to the monstrosity that crowned her. Forbearance and Christian patience may be exercised even on a toilette à la Louis XV. Long practice enabled her to walk about, seat herself, rise and curtsey without detriment to the edifice, or bestowing the powder either on her neighbours or on the richly-flowered white brocade she wore; while she received the compliments, one after another, of ladies in even more gorgeous array, and gentlemen in velvet coats, adorned with gold lace, cravats of exquisite fabric, and diamond shoe buckles.

Phelim Burke, otherwise l'Abbé de St. Eudoce, stood near her. He was a thin, yellow, and freckled youth, with sandy hair and typical Irish features, but without their drollery, and his face was what might have been expected in a half-starved, half-clad gossoon in a cabin, rather than surmounting a silken *soutane* in a Parisian salon; but he had a pleasant smile when kindly addressed by his friends.

Presently Lady Nithsdale drew near, accompanied by a tall, grave gentleman, and bringing with them a still taller youth, with the stiffest of backs and the longest of legs, who, when presented, made a bow apparently from the end of his spine, like Estelle's lamented Dutch-jointed doll when made to sit down. Moreover, he was more shabbily dressed than any other gentleman present, with a general outgrown look about his coat, and darns in his silk stockings; and though they were made by the hand of a Countess, that did not add to their elegance. And as he stood as stiff as a ramrod or as a sentinel, Estelle's good breeding was all called into play, and her mother's heart quailed as she said to herself, 'A great raw Scot! What can be done with him?

Lord Nithsdale spoke for him, thinking he had better go as secretary, and showing some handwriting of good quality. 'Did he know any languages?' 'French, English, Latin, and some Greek.' 'And, Madame,' added Lord Nithsdale, 'not only is his French much better than mine, as you would hear if the boy durst open his mouth, but our broad Scotch is so like Swedish that he will almost be an interpreter there.'

However hopeless Madame de Bourke felt, she smiled and professed herself rejoiced to hear it, and it was further decided that Arthur Maxwell Hope, aged eighteen, Scot by birth, should be mentioned among those of the Ambassador's household for whom she demanded passports. Her position rendered this no matter of difficulty, and it was wiser to give the full truth to the home authorities; but as it was desirable that it should not be reported to the English Government that Lord Burnside's brother was in the suite of the Jacobite Comte de Bourke, he was only to be known to the public by his first name, which was not much harder to French lips than Maxwell or Hope.

'Tall and black and awkward,' said Estelle, describing him to her brother. 'I shall not like him—I shall call him Phalante instead of Arthur.'

'Arthur,' said Ulysse; 'King Arthur was turned into a crow!'

'Well, this Arthur is like a crow—a great black skinny crow with torn feathers.'

CHAPTER III—ON THE RHONE

'Fairer scenes the opening eye
Of the day can scarce descry,
Fairer sight he looks not on
Than the pleasant banks of Rhone.'

ARCHBISHOP TRENCH.

Long legs may be in the abstract an advantage, but scarcely so in what was called in France *une grande Berline*. This was the favourite travelling carriage of the eighteenth century, and consisted of a close carriage or coach proper, with arrangements on the top for luggage, and behind it another seat open, but provided with a large leathern hood, and in front another place for the coachman and his companions. Each seat was wide enough to hold three persons, and thus within sat Madame de Bourke, her brother-in-law, the two children, Arthur Hope, and Mademoiselle Julienne, an elderly woman of the artisan class, *femme de chambre* to the Countess. Victorine, who was attendant on the children, would travel under the hood with two more maids; and the front seat would be occupied by the coachman, Laurence Callaghan— otherwise La Jeunesse, and Maître Hébert, the *maître d'hôtel*. Fain would Arthur have shared their elevation, so far as ease and comfort of mind and body went, and the Countess's wishes may have gone the same way; but besides that it would have been an insult to class him with the servants, the horses of the home establishment, driven by their own coachman, took the party the first stage out of Paris; and though afterwards the post-horses or mules, six in number, would be ridden by their own postilions, there was such an amount of luggage as to leave little or no space for a third person outside.

It had been a perfect sight to see the carriage packed; when Arthur, convoyed by Lord Nithsdale, arrived in the courtyard of the Hôtel de Varennes. Madame de Bourke was taking with her all the paraphernalia of an ambassador—a service of plate, in a huge chest stowed under the seat, a portrait of Philip V., in a gold frame set with diamonds, being included among her jewellery—and Lord Nithsdale, standing by, could not but drily remark, 'Yonder is more than we brought with us, Arthur.'

The two walked up and down the court together, unwilling to intrude on the parting which, as they well knew, would be made in floods of tears. Sad enough indeed it was, for Madame de Varennes was advanced in years, and her daughter had not only to part with her, but with the baby Jacques, for an unknown space of time; but the self-command and restraint of grief for the sake of each other was absolutely unknown. It was a point of honour and sentiment to weep as much as possible, and it would have been regarded as frigid and unnatural not to go on crying too much to eat or speak for a whole day beforehand, and at least two afterwards.

So when the travellers descended the steps to take their seats, each face was enveloped in a handkerchief, and there were passionate embraces, literal pressings to the breast, and violent sobs, as each victim, one after the other, ascended the carriage steps and fell back on the seat; while in the background, Honor Callaghan was uttering Irish wails over the Abbé and Laurence, and the lamentable sound set the little lap-dog and the big watch-dog howling in chorus. Arthur Hope, probably as miserable as any of them in parting with his friend and hero, was only standing like a stake, and an embarrassed stake (if that be possible), and Lord Nithsdale, though anxious for him, heartily pitying all, was nevertheless haunted by a queer recollection of Lance and his dog, and thinking that French dogs were not devoid of sympathy, and that the part of Crab was left for Arthur.

However, the last embrace was given, and the ladies were all packed in, while the Abbé with his breast heaving with sobs, his big hat in one hand, and a huge silk pocket-handkerchief in the other, did not forget his manners, but waved to Arthur to ascend the steps first. 'Secretary, not guest. You must remember that another time,' said Lord Nithsdale. 'God bless you, my dear lad, and bring you safe back to bonny Scotland, a true and leal heart.'

Arthur wrung his friend's hand once more, and disappeared into the vehicle; Nurse Honor made one more rush, and uttered another 'Ohone' over Abbé Phelim, who followed into the carriage; the door was shut; there was a last wail over 'Lanty, the sunbeam of me heart,' as he climbed to the box seat; the harness jingled; coachman and postilions cracked their whips, the impatient horses dashed out at the *porte cochére*; and Arthur, after endeavouring to dispose of his legs, looked about him, and saw, opposite to him, Madame de Bourke lying back in the corner in a transport of grief, one arm round her daughter, and her little son lying across her lap, both sobbing and crying; and on one side of him the Abbé, sunk in his corner, his yellow silk handkerchief over his face; on the other, Mademoiselle Julienne, who was crying too, but with more moderation, perhaps more out of propriety or from infection than from actual grief: at any rate she had more of her senses about her than any one else, and managed to dispose of the various loose articles that had been thrown after the travellers, in pockets and under cushions. Arthur would have assisted, but only succeeded in treading on various toes and eliciting some small shrieks, which disconcerted him all the more, and made Mademoiselle Julienne look daggers at him, as she relieved her lady of little Ulysse, lifting him to her own knee, where, as he was absolutely exhausted with crying, he fell asleep.

Arthur hoped the others would do the same, and perhaps there was more dozing than they would have confessed; but whenever there was a movement, and some familiar object in the streets of Paris struck the eye of Madame, the Abbé, or Estelle, there was a little cry, and they went off on a fresh score.

'Poor wretched weak creatures!' he said to himself, as he thought the traditions of Scottish heroic women in whose heroism he had gloated. And yet he was wrong: Madame de Bourke was capable of as much resolute self-devotion as any of the ladies on the other side of the Channel, but tears were a tribute required by the times. So she gave way to them—just as no doubt the women of former days saw nothing absurd in bottling them.

Arthur's position among all these weeping figures was extremely awkward, all the more so that he carried his sword upright between his legs, not daring to disturb the lachrymose company enough to dispose of it in the sword case appropriated to weapons. He longed to take out the little pocket Virgil, which Lord Nithsdale had given him, so as to have some occupation for his eyes, but he durst not, lest he should be thought rude, till, at a halt at a cabaret to water the horses, the striking of a clock reminded the Abbé that it was the time for reading the Hours, and when the breviary was taken out, Arthur thought his book might follow it.

By and by there was a halt at Corbeil, where was the nunnery of Alice Bourke, of whom her brother and sister-in-law were to take leave. They, with the children, were set down there, while Arthur went on with the carriage and servants to the inn to dine.

It was the first visit of Ulysse to the convent, and he was much amazed at peeping at his aunt's hooded face through a grating. However, the family were admitted to dine in the refectory; but poor Madame de Bourke was fit for nothing but to lie on a bed, attended affectionately by her sister-in-law, Soeur Ste. Madeleine.

'O sister, sister,' was her cry, 'I must say it to you—I would not to my poor mother—that I have the most horrible presentiments I shall never see her again, nor my poor child. No, nor my husband; I knew it when he took leave of me for that terrible Spain.'

'Yet you see he is safe, and you will be with him, sister,' returned the nun.

'Ah! that I knew I should! But think of those fearful Pyrenees, and the bandits that infest them—and all the valuables we carry with us!'

'Surely I heard that Marshal Berwick had offered you an escort.'

'That will only attract the attention of the brigands and bring them in greater force. O sister, sister, my heart sinks at the thought of my poor children in the hands of those savages! I dream of them every night.'

'The suite of an ambassador is sacred.'

'Ah! but what do they care for that, the robbers? I know destruction lies that way!'

'Nay, sister, this is not like you. You always were brave, and trusted heaven, when you had to follow Ulick.'

'Alas! never had I this sinking of heart, which tells me I shall be torn from my poor children and never rejoin him.'

Sister Ste. Madeleine caressed and prayed with the poor lady, and did her utmost to reassure and comfort her, promising a *neuvaine* for her safe journey and meeting with her husband.

'For the children,' said the poor Countess. 'I know I never shall see him more.'

However, the cheerfulness of the bright Irish-woman had done her some good, and she was better by the time she rose to pursue her journey. Estelle and Ulysse had been much petted by the nuns, and when all met again, to the great relief of Arthur, he found continuous weeping was not *de rigueur*. When they got in again, he was able to get rid of his sword, and only trod on two pair of toes, and got his legs twice tumbled over.

Moreover, Madame de Bourke had recovered the faculty of making pretty speeches, and when the weapon was put into the sword case, she observed with a sad little smile, 'Ah, Monsieur! we look to you as our defender!'

'And me too!' cried little Ulysse, making a violent demonstration with his tiny blade, and so nearly poking out his uncle's eye that the article was relegated to the same hiding-place as 'Monsieur Arture's,' and the boy was assured that this was a proof of his manliness.

He had quite recovered his spirits, and as his mother and sister were still exhausted with weeping, he was not easy to manage, till Arthur took heart of grace, and offering him a perch on his knee, let him look out at the window, explaining the objects on the way, which were all quite new to the little Parisian boy. Fortunately he spoke French well, with scarcely any foreign accent, and his answers to the little fellow's eager questions interspersed with observations on 'What they do in my country,' not only kept Ulysse occupied, but gained Estelle's attention, though she was too weary and languid, and perhaps, child as she was, too much bound by the requirements of sympathy to manifest her interest, otherwise than by moving near enough to listen.

That evening the party reached the banks of one of the canals which connected the rivers of France, and which was to convey them to the Loire and thence to the Rhone, in a huge flat-bottomed barge, called a *coche d'eau*, a sort of ark, with cabins, where travellers could be fairly comfortable, space where the berlin could be stowed away in the rear, and a deck with an awning where the passengers could disport themselves. From the days of Sully to those of the Revolution, this was by far the most convenient and secure mode of transport, especially in the south of France. It was very convenient to the Bourke party; who were soon established on the deck. The lady's dress was better adapted to travelling than the full costume of Paris. It was what she called *en Amazone*—namely, a clothe riding-habit faced with blue, with a short skirt, with open coat and waistcoat, like a man's, hair unpowdered and tied behind, and a large shady feathered hat. Estelle wore a miniature of the same, and rejoiced in her freedom from the whalebone stiffness of her Paris life, skipping about the deck with her brother, like fairies, Lanty said, or, as she preferred to make it, 'like a nymph.'

The water coach moved only by day, and was already arrived before the land one brought the weary party to the meeting-place—a picturesque water-side inn with a high roof, and a trellised passage down to the landing-place, covered by a vine, hung with clusters of ripe grapes.

Here the travellers supped on omelettes and *vin ordinaire*, and went off to bed —Madame and her child in one bed, with the maids on the floor, and in another room the Abbé and secretary, each in a *grabat*, the two men-servants in like manner, on the floor. Such was the privacy of the eighteenth century, and Arthur, used to waiting on himself, looked on with wonder to see the Abbé like a baby in the hands of his faithful foster-brother, who talked away in a queer mixture of Irish-English and French all the time until they knelt down and said their prayers together in Latin, to which Arthur diligently closed his Protestant ears.

Early the next morning the family embarked, the carriage having been already put on board; and the journey became very agreeable as they glided slowly, almost dreamily along, borne chiefly by the current, although a couple of horses towed the barge by a rope on the bank, in case of need, in places where the water was more sluggish, but nothing more was wanting in the descent towards the Mediterranean.

The accommodation was not of a high order, but whenever there was a halt near a good inn, Madame de Bourke and the children landed for the night. And in the fine days of early autumn the deck was delightful, and to dine there on the provisions brought on board was a perpetual feast to Estelle and Ulysse.

The weather was beautiful, and there was a constant panorama of fair sights and scenes. Harvest first, a perfectly new spectacle to the children and then, as they went farther south, the vintage. The beauty was great as they glided along the pleasant banks of Rhone.

Tiers of vines on the hillsides were mostly cut and trimmed like currant bushes, and disappointed Arthur, who had expected festoons on trellises. But this was the special time for beauty. The whole population, in picturesque costumes, were filling huge baskets with the clusters, and snatches of their merry songs came pealing down to the *coche d'eau*, as it quietly crept along. Towards evening groups were seen with piled baskets on their heads, or borne between them, youths and maidens crowned with vines, half-naked children dancing like little Bacchanalians, which awoke classical recollections in Arthur and delighted the children.

Poor Madame de Bourke was still much depressed, and would sit dreaming half the day, except when roused by some need of her children, some question, or some appeal for her admiration. Otherwise, the lovely heights, surmounted with tall towers, extinguisher-capped, of castle, convent, or church, the clear reaches of river, the beautiful turns, the little villages and towns gleaming white among the trees, seemed to pass unseen before her eyes, and she might be seen to shudder when the children pressed her to say how many days it would be before they saw their father.

An observer with a mind at ease might have been much entertained with the airs and graces that the two maids, Rosette and Babette, lavished upon Laurence, their only squire; for Maître Hébert was far too distant and elderly a person for their little coquetries. Rosette dealt in little terrors, and, if he was at hand, durst not step across a plank without his hand, was sure she heard wolves howling in the woods, and that every peasant was '*ce barbare*;' while Babette, who in conjunction with Maître Hébert acted cook in case of need, plied him with dainty morsels, which he was only too apt to bestow on the beggars, or the lean and hungry lad who attended on the horses. Victorine, on the other hand, by far the prettiest and most sprightly of the three, affected the most supreme indifference to him and his attentions, and hardly deigned to give him a civil word, or to accept the cornflowers and late roses he brought her from time to time. 'Mere weeds,' she said. And the grapes and Queen Claude plums he brought her were always sour. Yet a something deep blue might often be seen peeping above her trim little apron.

Not that Lanty had much time to disport himself in this fashion, for the Abbé was his care, and was perfectly happy with a rod of his arranging, with which to fish over the side. Little Ulysse was of course fired with the same emulation, and dangled his line for an hour together. Estelle would have liked to do the same, but her mother and Mademoiselle Julienne considered the sport not *convenable* for a *demoiselle*. Arthur was once or twice induced to try the Abbé's rod, but he found it as mere a toy as that of the boy; and the mere action of throwing it made his heart so sick with the contrast with the 'paidling in the burns' of his childhood, that he had no inclination to continue the attempt, either in the slow canal or the broadening river.

He was still very shy with the Countess, who was not in spirits to set him at ease; and the Abbé puzzled him, as is often the case when inexperienced strangers encounter unacknowledged deficiency. The perpetual coaxing chatter, and undisguised familiarity of La Jeunesse with the young ecclesiastic did not seem to the somewhat haughty cast of his young Scotch mind quite becoming, and he held aloof; but with the two children he was quite at ease, and was in truth their great resource.

He made Ulysse's fishing-rod, baited it, and held the boy when he used it— nay, he once even captured a tiny fish with it, to the ecstatic pity of both children. He played quiet games with them, and told them stories—conversed on Télémaque with Estelle, or read to her from his one book, which was Robinson Crusoe—a little black copy in pale print, with the margins almost thumbed away, which he had carried in his pocket when he ran away from school, and nearly knew by heart.

Estelle was deeply interested in it, and varied in opinion whether she should prefer Calypso's island or Crusoe's, which she took for as much matter of fact as did, a century later, Madame Talleyrand, when, out of civility to Mr. Robinson, she inquired after '*ce bon Vendredi.*'

She inclined to think she should prefer Friday to the nymphs.

'A whole quantity of troublesome womenfolk to fash one,' said Arthur, who had not arrived at the age of gallantry.

'You would never stay there!' said Estelle; 'you would push us over the rock like Mentor. I think you are our Mentor, for I am sure you tell us a great deal, and you don't scold.'

'Mentor was a cross old man,' said Ulysse.

To which Estelle replied that he was a goddess; and Arthur very decidedly disclaimed either character, especially the pushing over rocks. And thus they glided on, spending a night in the great, busy, bewildering city of Lyon, already the centre of silk industry; but more interesting to the travellers as the shrine of the martyrdoms. All went to pray at the Cathedral except Arthur. The time was not come for heeding church architecture or primitive history; and he only wandered about the narrow crooked streets, gazing at the toy piles of market produce, and looking at the stalls of merchandise, but as one unable to purchase. His mother had indeed contrived to send him twenty guineas, but he knew that he must husband them well in case of emergencies, and Lady Nithsdale had sewn them all up, except one, in a belt which he wore under his clothes.

He had arrived at the front of the Cathedral when the party came out. Madame de Bourke had been weeping, but looked more peaceful than he had yet seen her, and Estelle was much excited. She had bought a little book, which she insisted on her Mentor's reading with her, though his Protestant feelings recoiled.

'Ah!' said Estelle, 'but you are not Christian.'

'Yes, truly, Mademoiselle.'

'And these died for the Christian faith. Do you know mamma said it comforted her to pray there; for she was sure that whatever happened, the good God can make us strong, as He made the young girl who sat in the red-hot chair. We saw her picture, and it was dreadful. Do read about her, Monsieur Arture.'

They read, and Arthur had candour enough to perceive that this was the simple primitive narrative of the death of martyrs struggling for Christian truth, long ere the days of superstition and division. Estelle's face lighted with enthusiasm.

'Is it not noble to be a martyr?' she asked.

'Oh!' cried Ulysse; 'to sit in a red-hot chair! It would be worse than to be thrown off a rock! But there are no martyrs in these days, sister?' he added, pressing up to Arthur as if for protection.

'There are those who die for the right,' said Arthur, thinking of Lord Derwentwater, who in Jacobite eyes was a martyr.

'And the good God makes them strong,' said Estelle, in a low voice. 'Mamma told me no one could tell how soon we might be tried, and that I was to pray that He would make us as brave as St. Blandina! What do you think could harm us, Monsieur, when we are going to my dear papa?'

It was Lanty who answered, from behind the Abbé, on whose angling endeavours he was attending. 'Arrah then, nothing at all, Mademoiselle. Nothing in the four corners of the world shall hurt one curl of your blessed little head, while Lanty Callaghan is to the fore.'

'Ah! but you are not God, Lanty,' said Estelle gravely; 'you cannot keep things from happening.'

'The Powers forbid that I should spake such blasphemy!' said Lanty, taking off his hat. ''Twas not that I meant, but only that poor Lanty would die ten thousand deaths—worse than them as was thrown to the beasts—before one of them should harm the tip of that little finger of yours!'

Perhaps the same vow was in Arthur's heart, though not spoken in such

33

strong terms.

Thus they drifted on till the old city of Avignon rose on the eyes of the travellers, a dark pile of buildings where the massive houses, built round courts, with few external windows, recalled that these had once been the palaces of cardinals accustomed to the Italian city feuds, which made every house become a fortress.

On the wharf stood a gentleman in a resplendent uniform of blue and gold, whom the children hailed with cries of joy and outstretched arms, as their uncle. The Marquis de Varennes was soon on board, embracing his sister and her children, and conducting them to one of the great palaces, where he had rooms, being then in garrison. Arthur followed, at a sign from the lady, who presented him to her brother as 'Monsieur Arture'—a young Scottish gentleman who will do my husband the favour of acting as his secretary.

She used the word *gentilhomme*, which conveyed the sense of nobility of blood, and the Marquis acknowledged the introduction with one of those graceful bows that Arthur hated, because they made him doubly feel the stiffness of his own limitation. He was glad to linger with Lanty, who was looking in wonder at the grim buildings.

'And did the holy Father live here?' said he. 'Faith, and 'twas a quare taste he must have had; I wonder now if there would be vartue in a bit of a stone from his palace. It would mightily please my old mother if there were.'

'I thought it was the wrong popes that lived here,' suggested Arthur.

Lanty looked at him a moment as if in doubt whether to accept a heretic suggestion, but the education received through the Abbé came to mind, and he exclaimed—

'May be you are in the right of it, sir; and I'd best let the stones alone till I can tell which is the true and which is the false. By the same token, little is the difference it would make to her, unless she knew it; and if she did, she'd as soon I brought her a hair of the old dragon's bristles.'

Lanty found another day or two's journey bring him very nearly in contact with the old dragon, for at Tarascon was the cave in which St. Martha was said to have demolished the great dragon of Provence with the sign of the cross. Madame de Bourke and her children made a devout pilgrimage thereto; but when Arthur found that it was the actual Martha of Bethany to whom the legend was appended, he grew indignant, and would not accompany the party. 'It was a very different thing from the martyrs of Lyon and Vienne! Their history was credible, but this—'

'Speak not so loud, my friend,' said M. de Varennes. 'Their shrines are equally good to console women and children.'

Arthur did not quite understand the tone, nor know whether to be gratified at being treated as a man, or to be shocked at the Marquis's defection from his own faith.

The Marquis, who was able to accompany his sister as far as Montpelier, was amused at her two followers, Scotch and Irish, both fine young men—almost too fine, he averred.

'You will have to keep a careful watch on them when you enter Germany, sister,' he said, 'or the King of Prussia will certainly kidnap them for his tall regiment of grenadiers.'

'O brother, do not speak of any more dangers: I see quite enough before me ere I can even rejoin my dear husband.'

A very serious council was held between the brother and sister. The French army under Marshal Berwick had marched across on the south side on the Pyrenees, and was probably by this time in the county of Rousillon, intending to besiege Rosas. Once with them all would be well, but between lay the mountain roads, and the very quarter of Spain that had been most unwilling to accept French rule.

The Marquis had been authorised to place an escort at his sister's service, but though the numbers might guard her against mere mountain banditti, they would not be sufficient to protect her from hostile troops, such as might only too possibly be on the way to encounter Berwick. The expense and difficulty of the journey on the mountain roads would likewise be great, and it seemed advisable to avoid these dangers by going by sea. Madame de Bourke eagerly acceded to this plan, her terror of the wild Pyrenean passes and wilder inhabitants had always been such that she was glad to catch at any means of avoiding them, and she had made more than one voyage before.

Estelle was gratified to find they were to go by sea, since Télémachus did so in a Phoenician ship, and, in that odd dreamy way in which children blend fiction and reality, wondered if they should come on Calypso's island; and Arthur, who had read the Odyssey, delighted her and terrified Ulysse with the cave of Polyphemus. M. de Varennes could only go with his sister as far as Montpelier. Then he took leave of her, and the party proceeded along the shores of the lagoons, in the carriage to the seaport of Cette, one of the old Greek towns of the Gulf of Lyon, and with a fine harbour full of ships. Maître Hébert was sent to take a passage on board of one, while his lady and her party repaired to an inn, and waited all the afternoon before he returned with tidings that he could find no French vessel about to sail for Spain, but that there was a Genoese tartane, bound for Barcelona, on which Madame la

Comtesse could secure a passage for herself and her suite, and which would take her thither in twenty-four hours.

The town was full of troops, waiting a summons to join Marshal Berwick's army. Several resplendent officers had already paid their respects to Madame l'Ambassadrice, and they concurred in the advice, unless she would prefer waiting for the arrival of one of the French transports which were to take men and provisions to the army in Spain.

This, however, she declined, and only accepted the services of the gentlemen so far as to have her passports renewed, as was needful, since they were to be conveyed by the vessel of an independent power, though always an ally of France.

The tartane was a beautiful object, a one-decked, single-masted vessel, with a long bowsprit, and a huge lateen sail like a wing, and the children fell in love with her at first sight. Estelle was quite sure that she was just such a ship as Mentor borrowed for Télémachus; but the poor maids were horribly frightened, and Babette might be heard declaring she had never engaged herself to be at the mercy of the waves, like a bit of lemon peel in a glass of *eau sucrée*.

'You may return,' said Madame de Bourke. 'I compel no one to share our dangers and hardships.'

But Babette threw herself on her knees, and declared that nothing should ever separate her from Madame! She was a good creature, but she could not deny herself the luxury of the sobs and tears that showed to all beholders the extent of her sacrifice.

Madame de Bourke knew that there would be considerable discomfort in a vessel so little adapted for passengers, and with only one small cabin, which the captain, who spoke French, resigned to her use. It would only, however, be for a short time, and though it was near the end of October, the blue expanse of sea was calm as only the Mediterranean can be, so that she trusted that no harm would result to those who would have to spend the night on dock.

It was a beautiful evening which the little Genoese vessel left the harbour and Cette receded in the distance, looking fairer the farther it was left behind. The children were put to bed as soon as they could be persuaded to cease from watching the lights in the harbour and the phosphorescent wake of the vessel in the water.

That night and the next day were pleasant and peaceful; there was no rough weather, and little sickness among the travellers. Madame de Bourke congratulated herself on having escaped the horrors of the Pyrenean journey, and the Genoese captain assured her that unless the weather should change rapidly, they would wake in sight of the Spanish coast the next morning. If the sea were not almost too calm, they would be there already. The evening was again so delightful that the children were glad to hear that they would have again to return by sea, and Arthur, who somewhat shrank from his presentation to the Count, regretted that the end of the voyage was so near, though Ulysse assured him that '*Mon papa* would love him, because he could tell such charming stories,' and Lanty testified that 'M. le Comte was a mighty friendly gentleman.'

Arthur was lying asleep on deck, wrapped in his cloak, when he was awakened by a commotion among the sailors. He started up and found that it was early morning, the sun rising above the sea, and the sailors all gazing eagerly in that direction. He eagerly made his way to ask if they were in sight of land, recollecting, however, as he made the first step, that Spain lay to the west of them—not to the east.

He distinguished the cry from the Genoese sailors, '*Ii Moro—Il Moro,*' in tones of horror and consternation, and almost at the same moment received a shock from Maître Hébert, who came stumbling against him.

'Pardon, pardon, Monsieur; I go to prepare Madame! It's the accursed Moors. Let me pass—*miséricorde*, what will become of us?'

Arthur struggled on in search of such of the crew as could speak French, but all were in too much consternation to attend to him, and he could only watch that to which their eyes were directed, a white sail, bright in the morning light, coming up with a rapidity strange and fearful in its precision, like a hawk pouncing on its prey, for it did not depend on its sails alone, but was propelled by oars.

The next moment Madame de Bourke was on deck, holding by the Abbé's arm, and Estelle, her hair on her shoulders, clinging to her. She looked very pale, but her calmness was in contrast to the Italian sailors, who were throwing themselves with gestures of despair, screaming out vows to the Madonna and saints, and shouting imprecations. The skipper came to speak to her. 'Madame,' he said, 'I implore you to remain in your cabin. After the first, you and all yours will be safe. They cannot harm a French subject; alas! alas would it were so with us.'

'How then will it be with you?' she asked.

He made a gesture of deprecation.

'For me it will be ruin; for my poor fellows slavery; that is, if we survive the onset. Madame, I entreat of you, take shelter in the cabin, yourself and all yours. None can answer for what the first rush of these fiends may be! *Diavoli! veri diavola!* Ah! for which of my sins is it that after fifty voyages I should be condemned to lose my all?'

A fresh outburst of screams from the crew summoned the captain. 'They are putting out the long-boat,' was the cry; 'they will board us!'

'Madame! I entreat of you, shut yourself into the cabin.'

And the four maids in various stages of *déshabille*, adding their cries to those of the sailors, tried to drag her in, but she looked about for Arthur. 'Come with us, Monsieur,' she said quietly, for after all her previous depressions and alarms, her spirit rose to endurance in the actual stress of danger. 'Come with us, I entreat of you,' she said. 'You are named in our passports, and the treaties are such that neither French nor English subjects can be maltreated nor enslaved by these wretches. As the captain says, the danger is only in the first attack.'

'I will protect you, Madame, with my life,' declared Arthur, drawing his sword, as his cheeks and eyes lighted.

'Ah, put that away. What could you do but lose your own?' cried the lady. 'Remember, you have a mother—'

The Genoese captain here turned to insist that Madame and all the women should shut themselves instantly into the cabin. Estelle dragged hard at Arthur's hand, with entreaties that he would come, but he lifted her down the ladder, and then closed the door on her, Lanty and he being both left outside.

'To be shut into a hole like a rat in a trap when there's blows to the fore, is more than flesh could stand,' said Lanty, who had seized on a hand-spike and was waving it about his head, true shillelagh fashion, by hereditary instinct in one who had never behold a faction fight, in what ought to have been his native land.

The Genoese captain looked at him as a madman, and shouted in a confused mixture of French and Italian to lay down his weapon.

'*Quei cattivi—ces scelerats* were armed to the teeth—would fire. All lie flat on the deck.'

The gesture spoke for itself. With a fearful howl all the Italians dropped flat; but neither Scotch nor Irish blood brooked to follow their example, or perhaps fully perceived the urgency of the need, till a volley of bullets were whistling about their ears, though happily without injury, the mast and the rigging having protected them, for the sail was riddled with holes, and the smoke dimmed their vision as the report sounded in their ears. In another second the turbaned, scimitared figures were leaping on board. The Genoese still lay flat offering no resistance, but Lanty and Arthur stood on either side of the ladder, and hurled back the two who first approached; but four or five more rushed upon them, and they would have been instantly cut down, had it not been for a shout from the Genoese, '*Franchi! Franchi!*' At that magic word, which was evidently understood, the pirates only held the two youths tightly, vituperating them no doubt in bad Arabic,—Lanty grinding his teeth with rage, though scarcely feeling the pain of the two sabre cuts he had received, and pouring forth a volley of exclamations, chiefly, however, directed against the white-livered spalpeens of sailors, who had not lifted so much as a hand to help him. Fortunately no one understood a word he said but Arthur, who had military experience enough to know there was nothing for it but to stand still in the grasp of his captor, a wiry-looking Moor, with a fez and a striped sash round his waist.

The leader, a sturdy Turk in a dirty white turban, with a huge sabre in his hand, was listening to the eager words, poured out with many gesticulations by the Genoese captain, in a language utterly incomprehensible to the Scot, but which was the *lingua França* of the Mediterranean ports.

It resulted in four men being placed on guard at the hatchway leading to the cabin, while all the rest, including Arthur, Hébert, Laurence, were driven toward the prow, and made to understand by signs that they must not move on peril of their lives. A Tuck was placed at the helm, and the tartane's head turned towards the pirate captor; and all the others, who were not employed otherwise, began to ransack the vessel and feast on the provisions. Some hams were thrown overboard, with shouts of evident scorn as belonging to the unclean beast, but the wine was eagerly drank, and Maître Hébert uttered a wail of dismay as he saw five Moors gorging large pieces of his finest *pâté*.

CHAPTER IV—WRECKED

'They had na sailed upon the sea
  A day but barely three,
When the lift grew dark and the wind blew cauld
  And gurly grew the sea.

'Oh where will I find a little wee boy
  Will tak my helm in hand,
Till I gae up to my top mast
  And see for some dry land.'

SIR PATRICK SPENS.

It was bad enough on the deck of the unfortunate Genoese tartane, but far worse below, where eight persons were shut into the stifling atmosphere of the cabin, deprived of the knowledge of what was going on above, except from the terrific sounds they heard. Estelle, on being shut into the cabin, announced that the Phoenician ship was taken by the vessels of Sesostris, but this did not afford any one else the same satisfaction as she appeared to derive from it. Babette and Rosette were echoing every scream of the crew, and quite certain that all would be massacred, and little Ulysse, wakened by the hubbub, rolled round in his berth and began to cry.

Madame de Bourke, very white, but quite calm, insisted on silence and then said, 'I do not think the danger is very great to ourselves if you will keep silence and not attract attention. But our hope is in Heaven. My brother, will you lead our prayers? Recite our office.' Obediently the Abbé fell on his knees, and his example was followed by the others. His voice went monotonously on throughout with the Latin. The lady, no doubt, followed in her heart, and she made the responses as did the others, fitfully; but her hands and eyes were busy, looking to the priming of two small pistols, which she took out of her jewel case, and the sight of which provoked fresh shrieks from the maids. Mademoiselle Julienne meantime was dressing Ulysse, and standing guard over him, Estelle watching all with eager bright eyes, scarcely frightened, but burning to ask questions, from which her uncle's prayers debarred her.

At the volley of shot, Rosette was reduced to quiet by a swoon, but Victorine, screaming that the wretches would have killed Laurent, would have rushed on deck, had not her mistress forcibly withheld her. There ensued a prodigious

41

yelling and howling, trampling and scuffling, then the sounds of strange languages in vituperation or command, steps coming down the ladder, sounds of altercation, retreat, splashes in the sea, the feeling that the ship was put about—and ever the trampling, the wild cries of exultation, which over and over again made the prisoners feel choked with the horror of some frightful crisis close at hand. And all the time they were in ignorance, their little window in the stern showed them nothing but sea; and even if Madame de Bourke's determination had not hindered Victorine from peeping out of the cabin, whether prison or fortress, the Moorish sentries outside kept the door closed.

How long this continued was scarcely to be guessed. It was hours by their own feelings; Ulysse began to cry from hunger, and his mother gave him and Estelle some cakes that were within reach. Mademoiselle Julienne begged her lady to share the repast, reminding her that she would need all her strength. The Abbé, too, was hungry enough, and some wine and preserved fruits coming to light all the prisoners made a meal which heartened most of them considerably; although the heat was becoming terrible, as the sun rose higher in the sky, and very little air could be obtained through the window, so that poor Julienne could not eat, and Rosette fell into a heavy sleep in the midst of her sighs. Even Estelle, who had got out her Télémaque, like a sort of oracle in the course of being verified, was asleep over it, when fresh noises and grating sounds were board, new steps on deck, and there were steps and voices. The Genoese captain was heard exclaiming, 'Open, Madame! you can do so safely. This is the Algerine captain, who is bound to protect you.'

The maids huddled together behind their lady, who stood forward as the door opened to admit a stout, squarely-built man in the typical dress of a Turk,— white turban, purple coat, broad sash crammed with weapons, and ample trousers,—a truculent-looking figure which made the maids shudder and embrace one another with suppressed shrieks, but which somehow, even in the midst of his Eastern salaam, gave the Countess a sense that he was acting a comedy, and carried her involuntarily back to the Moors whom she had seen in the *Cid* on the stage. And looking again, she perceived that though brown and weather-beaten, there was a certain Northern ruddiness inherent in his complexion; that his eyes were gray, so far as they were visible between the surrounding puckers; and his eyebrows, moustache, and beard not nearly so dark as the hair of the Genoese who stood cringing beside him as interpreter. She formed her own conclusions and adhered to them, though he spoke in bad Arabic to the skipper, who proceeded to explain that El Reis Hamed would offer no injury to Madame la Comtesse, her suite or property, being bound by treaty between the Dey and the King of France, but that he required to see her passport. There was a little blundering in the Italian's French rendering, and

Madame de Bourke was quick to detect the perception of it in the countenance of the Reis, stolid though it was. She felt no doubt that he was a renegade of European birth, and watched, with much anxiety as well as curiosity, his manner of dealing with her passports, which she would not let out of her own hand. She saw in a moment that though he let the Genoese begin to interpret them, his eyes were following intelligently; and she hazarded the observation, 'You understand, sir. You are Frank.'

He turned one startled glance towards the door to see if there were any listeners, and answered, 'Hollander, Madame.'

The Countess had travelled with diplomatists all her life, and knew a little of the vernacular of most languages, and it was in Dutch—broken indeed, but still Dutch—that she declared that she was sure that she might rely on his protection—a security which in truth she was far from feeling; for while some of these unfortunate men, renegades only from weakness, yearned after their compatriots and their lost home and faith, others out-heroded the Moors themselves in ferocity, especially towards the Christian captives; nor was a Dutchman likely to have any special tenderness in his composition, above all towards the French. However, there was a certain smile on the lips of Reis Hamed, and he answered with a very hearty, 'Ja! ja! Madame. Upon my soul I will let no harm come to you or the pretty little ones, nor the young vrouwkins either, if they will keep close. You are safe by treaty. A Reis would have to pay a heavy reckoning with Mehemed Dey if a French ambassador had to complain of him, and you will bear me witness, Madame, that I have not touched a hair of any of your heads!'

'I am sure you wish me well, sir,' said Madame de Bourke in a dignified way, 'but I require to be certified of the safety of the rest of my suite, my steward, my lackey, and my husband's secretary, a young gentleman of noble birth.'

'They are safe, Madame. This Italian slave can bear me witness that no creature has been harmed since my crew boarded this vessel.'

'I desire then that they may be released, as being named in my passport.'

To this the Dutchman consented.

Whereupon the skipper began to wring his hands, and piteously to beseech Madame to intercede for him, but the Dutchman cut him short before she could speak. 'Dog of an Italian, the lady knows better! You and your fellows are our prize—poor enough after all the trouble you have given us in chasing you.'

Madame de Bourke spoke kindly to the poor man, telling him that though she could do nothing for him now, it was possible that she might when she should have rejoined her husband, and she then requested the Reis to land her and her suite in his long-boat on the Spanish coast, which could be seen in the distance, promising him ample reward if he could do so.

To this he replied: 'Madame, you ask what would be death to me.'

He went on to explain that if he landed her on Christian ground, without first presenting her and her passport to the Dey and the French Consul, his men might represent him as acting in the interests of the Christians, and as a traitor to the Algerine power, by taking a bribe from a person belonging to a hostile state, in which case the bowstring would be the utmost mercy he could expect; and the reigning Dey, Mehemed, having been only recently chosen, it was impossible to guess how he might deal with such cases. Once at Algiers, he assured Madame de Bourke that she would have nothing to fear, as she would be under the protection of the French Consul; and she had no choice but to submit, though much concerned for the continued anxiety to her husband, as well as the long delay and uncertainty of finding him.

Still, when she perceived that it was inevitable, she complained no more, and the Dutchman went on with a certain bluff kindness—as one touched by her courtesy—to offer her the choice of remaining in the tartane or coming on board his larger vessel. The latter he did not recommend, as he had a crew of full two hundred Turks and Moors, and it would be necessary to keep herself and all her women as closely as possible secluded in the cabins; and even then, he added, that if once seen he could hardly answer for some of those corsairs not endeavouring to secure a fair young Frank girl for his harem; and as his eye fell on Rosette, she bridled and hid herself behind Mademoiselle Julienne.

He must, he said, remove all the Genoese, but he would send on board the tartane only seven men on whom he could perfectly depend for respectful behaviour, so that the captives would be able to take the air on deck as freely as before. There was no doubt that he was in earnest, and the lady accepted his offer with thanks, all the stronger since she and all around her were panting and sick for want of fresh air.

It was a great relief when he took her on deck with him that she might identify the three men whom she claimed as belonging to her suite. Arthur, Lanty, and Hébert, who, in their vague knowledge of the circumstances, had been dreading the oar for the rest of their lives, could hardly believe their good fortune when she called them up to her, and the Abbé gripped Lanty's arm as if he would never let him go again. The poor Italians seemed to feel their fate all the harder for the deliverance of those three, and sobbed, howled, and wept so piteously that Arthur wondered how strong men could so give way, while Lanty's tears sprang forth in sympathy, and he uttered assurances and made signs that he would never cease to pray for their rescue.

'Though,' as he observed, 'they were poor creatures that hadn't the heart of a midge, when there was such a chance of a fight while the haythen spalpeens were coming on board.'

Here Lanty was called on to assist Hébert in identifying his lady's bales of goods, when all those of the unfortunate Genoese were put on board the corsair's vessel. A sail-cloth partition was extended across the deck by the care of the Dutchman, 'who'—as Lanty said—'for a haythen apostate was a very dacent man.' He evidently had a strong compassion and fellow-feeling for the Christian lady, and assured her that she might safely take the air and sit on deck as much as she pleased behind its shelter; and he likewise carefully selected the seven of his crew whom he sent on board to work the ship, the chief being a heavy-looking old Turk, with a chocolate-coloured visage between a huge white beard and eyebrows, and the others mere lads, except one, who, from an indefinable European air about him, was evidently a renegade, and could speak a sort of French, so as to hold communication with the captives, especially Lanty, who was much quicker than any of the rest in picking up languages, perhaps from having from his infancy talked French and English (or rather Irish), and likewise learnt Latin with his foster-brother. This man was the only one permitted to go astern of the partition, in case of need, to attend to the helm; but the vessel was taken in tow by the corsair, and needed little management. The old Turk seemed to regard the Frankish women like so many basilisks, and avoided turning a glance in their direction, roaring at his crew if he only saw them approaching the sail-cloth, and keeping a close watch upon the lithe black-eyed youths, whose brown limbs carried them up the mast with the agility of monkeys. There was one in especial—a slight, well-made fellow about twenty, with a white turban cleaner than the rest—who contrived to cast wonderful glances from the masthead over the barrier at Rosette, who actually smiled in return at *ce pauvre garçon*, and smiled the more for Mademoiselle Julienne's indignation. Suddenly, however, a shrill shout made him descend hastily, and the old Turk's voice might be heard in its highest key, no doubt shrieking out maledictions on all the ancestry of the son of a dog who durst defile his eyes with gazing at the shameless daughters of the Frank. Little Ulysse was, however, allowed to disport himself wherever he pleased; and after once, under Arthur's protection, going forward, he found himself made very welcome, and offered various curiosities, such as shells, corals, and a curious dried little hippocampus or seahorse.

This he brought back in triumph, to the extreme delight of his sister's classical mind. 'Oh mamma, mamma,' she cried, 'Ulysse really has got the skeleton of a Triton. It is exactly like the stone creatures in the Champs Elysées.'

There was no denying the resemblance, and it so increased the confusion in Estelle's mind between the actual and the mythological, that Arthur told her that she was looking out for the car of Amphitrite to arise from the waters. Anxiety and trouble had made him much better acquainted with Madame de Bourke, who was grateful to him for his kindness to her children, and not without concern as to whether she should be able to procure his release as well as her own at Algiers. For Laurence Callaghan she had no fears, since he was born at Paris, and a naturalised French subject like her husband and his brother; but Arthur was undoubtedly a Briton, and unless she could pass him off as one of her suite, it would depend on the temper of the English Consul whether he should be viewed as a subject or as a rebel, or simply left to captivity until his Scottish relations should have the choice of ransoming him.

She took a good deal of pains to explain the circumstances to him as well as to all who could understand them; for though she hoped to keep all together, and to be able to act for them herself, no one could guess how they might be separated, and she could not shake off that foreboding of misfortune which had haunted her from the first.

The kingdom of Algiers was, she told them, tributary to the Turkish Sultan, who kept a guard of Janissaries there, from among whom they themselves elected the Dey. He was supposed to govern by the consent of a divan, but was practically as despotic as any Eastern sovereign; and the Aga of the Janissaries was next in authority to him. Piracy on the Mediterranean was, as all knew, the chief occupation of the Turks and Moors of any spirit or enterprise, a Turk being in authority in each vessel to secure that the Sultan had his share, and that the capture was so conducted as not to involve Turkey in dangerous wars with European powers. Capture by the Moors had for several centuries been one of the ordinary contingencies of a voyage, and the misfortune that had happened to the party was not at all an unusual one.

In 1687, however, the nuisance had grown to such a height that Admiral Du Quesne bombarded the town of Algiers, and destroyed all the fortifications, peace being only granted on condition that a French Consul should reside at Algiers, and that French ships and subjects should be exempt from this violence of the corsairs.

The like treaties existed with the English, but had been very little heeded by the Algerines till recently, when the possession of Gibraltar and Minorca had provided harbours for British ships, which exercised a salutary supervision over these Southern sea-kings. The last Dey, Baba Hali, had been a wise and prudent man, anxious to repress outrage, and to be on good terms with the two great European powers; but he had died in the spring of the current year, 1718, and the temper of his successor, Mehemed, had not yet been proved.

Madame de Bourke had some trust in the Dutch Reis, renegade though he was. She had given him her beautiful watch, set with brilliants, and he had taken it with a certain gruff reluctance, declaring that he did not want it,—he was ready enough to serve her without such a toy.

Nevertheless the lady thought it well to impress on each and all, in case of any separation or further disaster, that their appeal must be to the French Consul, explaining minutely the forms in which it should be made.

'I cannot tell you,' she said to Arthur, 'how great a comfort it is to me to have with me a gentleman, one of intelligence and education to whom I can confide my poor children. I know you will do your utmost to protect them and restore them to their father.'

'With my very heart's blood, Madame.'

'I hope that may not be asked of you, Monsieur,' she returned with a faint smile,—'though I fear there may be much of perplexity and difficulty in the way before again rejoining him. You see where I have placed our passports? My daughter knows it likewise; but in case of their being taken from you, or any other accident happening to you, I have written these two letters, which you had better bear about your person. One is, as you see, to our Consul at Algiers, and may serve as credentials; the other is to my husband, to whom I have already written respecting you.'

'A thousand thanks, Madame,' returned Arthur. 'But I hope and trust we may all reach M. le Comte in safety together. You yourself said that you expected only a brief detention before he could be communicated with, and this captain, renegade though he be, evidently has a respect for you.'

'That is quite true,' she returned, 'and it may only be my foolish heart that forebodes evil; nevertheless, I cannot but recollect that *c'est l'imprévu qui arrive.*'

'Then, Madame, that is the very reason there should be no misfortune,' returned Arthur.

It was on the second day after the capture of the tartane that the sun set in a purple angry-looking bank of cloud, and the sea began to heave in a manner which renewed the earlier distresses of the voyage to such as were bad sailors. The sails both of the corsair and of the tartane were taken in, and it was plain that a rough night was to be expected. The children were lashed into their berths, and all prepared themselves to endure. The last time Arthur saw Madame de Bourke's face, by the light of the lamp swinging furiously from the cabin roof, as he assisted in putting in the dead lights, it bore the same fixed expression of fortitude and resignation as when she was preparing to be boarded by the pirates.

He remained on deck, but it was very perilous, for the vessel was so low in the water that the waves dashed over it so wildly that he could hardly help being swept away. It was pitch dark, too, and the lantern of the other vessel could only just be seen, now high above their heads, now sinking in the trouble of the sea, while the little tartane was lifted up as though on a mountain; and in a kind of giddy dream, he thought of falling headlong upon her deck. Finally he found himself falling. Was he washed overboard? No; a sharp blow showed him that he had only fallen down the hatchway, and after lying still a moment, he heard the voices of Lanty and Hébert, and presently they were all tossed together by another lurch of the ship.

It was a night of miseries that seemed endless, and when a certain amount of light appeared, and Arthur and Lanty crawled upon deck, the tempest was unabated. They found themselves still dashed, as if their vessel were a mere cork, on the huge waves; rushes of water coming over them, whether from sea or sky there was no knowing, for all seemed blended together in one mass of dark lurid gray; and where was the Algerine ship—so lately their great enemy, now watched for as their guide and guardian?

It was no place nor time for questions, even could they have been heard or understood. It was scarcely possible even to be heard by one another, and it was some time before they convinced themselves that the large vessel had disappeared. The cable must have parted in the night, and they were running with bare poles before the gale; the seamanship of the man at the helm being confined to avoiding the more direct blows of the waves, on the huge crests of which the little tartane rode—gallantly perhaps in mariners' eyes, but very wretchedly to the feelings of the unhappy landsmen within her.

Arthur thought of St. Paul, and remembered with dismay that it was many days before sun or moon appeared. He managed to communicate his recollection to Lanty, who exclaimed, 'And he was a holy man, and he was a prisoner too. He will feel for us if any man can in this sore strait! *Sancte Paule, ora pro nobis.* An' haven't I got the blessed scapulary about me neck that will bring me through worse than this?'

The three managed to get down to tell the unfortunate inmates of the cabin what was the state of things, and to carry them some food, though at the expense of many falls and severe blows; and almost all of them were too faint or nauseated to be able to swallow such food as could survive the transport under such circumstances. Yet high-spirited little Estelle entreated to be carried on deck, to see what a storm was like. She had read of them so often, and wanted to see as well as to feel. She was almost ready to cry when Arthur assured her it was quite impossible, and her mother added a grave order not to trouble him.

Madame de Bourke looked so exhausted by the continual buffeting and the closeness of the cabin, and her voice was so weak, that Arthur grieved over the impossibility of giving her any air. Julienne tried to make her swallow some *eau de vie*; but the effort of steadying her hand seemed too much for her, and after a terrible lurch of the ship, which lodged the poor *bonne* in the opposite corner of the cabin, the lady shook her head and gave up the attempt. Indeed, she seemed so worn out that Arthur—little used to the sight of fainting—began to fear that her forebodings of dying before she could rejoin her husband were on the point of being realised.

However, the gale abated towards evening, and the youth himself was so much worn out that the first respite was spent in sleep. When he awoke, the sea was much calmer, and the eastern sun was rising in glory over it; the Turks, with their prayer carpets in a line, were simultaneously kneeling and bowing in prayer, with their faces turned towards it. Lanty uttered an only too emphatic curse upon the misbelievers, and Arthur vainly tried to make him believe that their 'Allah il Allah' was neither addressed to Mohammed nor the sun.

'Sure and if not, why did they make their obeisance to it all one as the Persians in the big history-book Master Phelim had at school?'

'It's to the east they turn Lanty, not to the sun.'

'And what right have the haythen spalpeens to turn to the east like good Christians?'

''Tis to their Prophet's tomb they look, at Mecca.'

'There, an' I tould you they were no better than haythens,' returned Lanty, 'to be praying and knocking their heads on the bare boards—that have as much sense as they have—to a dead man's tomb.'

Arthur's Scotch mind thought the Moors might have had the best of it in argument when he recollected Lanty's trust in his scapulary.

They tried to hold a conversation with the Reis, between *lingua Franca* and the Provençal of the renegade; and they came to the conclusion that no one had the least idea where they were, or where they were going; the ship's compass had been broken in the boarding, and there was no chart more available than the little map in the beginning of Estelle's precious copy of Télémaque. The Turkish Reis did not trouble himself about it, but squatted himself down with his chibouque, abandoning all guidance of the ship, and letting her drift at the will of wind and wave, or, as he said, the will of Allah. When asked where he thought she was going, he replied with solemn indifference, 'Kismet;' and all the survivors of the crew—for one had been washed overboard—seemed to share his resignation.

The only thing he did seem to care for was that if the infidel woman chose to persist in coming on deck, the canvas screen—which had been washed overboard—should be restored. This was done, and Madame de Bourke was assisted to a couch that had been prepared for her with cloaks, where the air revived her a little; but she listened with a faint smile to the assurances of Arthur, backed by Hébert, that this abandonment to fate gave the best chance. They might either be picked up by a Christian vessel or go ashore on a Christian coast; but Madame de Bourke did not build much on these hopes. She knew too well what were the habits of wreckers of all nations, to think that it would make much difference whether they were driven on the coast of Sicily or of Africa—'barring,' as Lanty said, 'that they should get Christian burial in the former case.'

'We are in the hands of a good God. That at least we know,' said the Countess. 'And He can hear us through, whether for life in Paradise, or trial a little longer here below.'

'Like Blandina,' observed Estelle.

'Ah! my child, who knows whether trials like even that blessed saint's may not be in reserve even for your tender age. When I think of these miserable men, who have renounced their faith, I see what fearful ordeals there may be for those who fall into the hands of those unbelievers. Strong men have yielded. How may it not be with my poor children?'

'God made Blandina brave, mamma. I will pray that He may make me so.'

Land was in sight at last. Purple mountains rose to the south in wild forms, looking strangely thunderous and red in the light of the sinking sun. A bay, with rocks jutting out far into the sea, seemed to embrace them with its arms. Soundings were made, and presently the Reis decided on anchoring. It was a rocky coast, with cliffs descending into the sea, covered with verdure, and the water beneath was clear as glass.

'Have we escaped the Syrtes to fall upon Æneas' cave?' murmured Arthur to himself.

'And if we could meet Queen Dido, or maybe Venus herself, 'twould be no bad thing!' observed Lanty, who remembered his Virgil on occasion. 'For there's not a drop of wather left barring *eau de vie*, and if these Moors get at that, 'tis raving madmen they would be.'

'Do they know where we are?' asked Arthur.

'Sorrah a bit!' returned Lanty, 'tho' 'tis a pretty place enough. If my old mother was here, 'tis her heart would warm to the mountains.'

'Is it Calypso's Island?' whispered Ulysse to his sister.

'See, what are they doing?' cried Estelle. 'There are people—don't you see, white specks crowding down to the water.'

There was just then a splash, and two bronzed figures were seen setting forth from the tartane to swim to shore. The Turkish Reis had despatched them, to ascertain whether the vessel had drifted, and who the inhabitants might be.

A good while elapsed before one of these scouts returned. There was a great deal of talk and gesticulating round him, and Lanty, mingling with it, brought back word that the place was the Bay of Golo, not far from Djigheli, and just beyond the Algerine frontier. The people were Cabeleyzes, a wild race of savage dogs, which means dogs according the Moors, living in the mountains, and independent of the Dey. A considerable number rushed to the coast, armed, and in great numbers, perceiving the tartane to be an Italian vessel, and expecting a raid by Sicilian robbers on their cattle; but the Moors had informed them that it was no such thing, but a prize taken in the name of the Dey of Algiers, in which an illustrious French Bey's harem was being conveyed to Algiers. From that city the tartane was now about a day's sail, having been driven to the eastward of it during the storm. 'The Turkish commander evidently does not like the neighbourhood,' said Arthur, 'judging by his gestures.'

'Dogs and sons of dogs are the best names he has for them,' rejoined Lanty.

'See! They have cut the cable! Are we not to wait for the other man who swam ashore?'

So it was. A favourable wind was blowing, and the Reis, being by no means certain of the disposition of the Cabeleyzes, chose to leave them behind him as soon as possible, and make his way to Algiers, which began to appear to his unfortunate passengers like a haven of safety.

They were not, however, out of the bay when the wind suddenly veered, and before the great lateen sail could be reefed, it had almost caused the vessel to be blown over. There was a pitching and tossing almost as violent as in the storm, and then wind and current began carrying the tartane towards the rocky shore. The Reis called the men to the oars, but their numbers were too few to be availing, and in a very few minutes more the vessel was driven hopelessly towards a mass of rocks.

Arthur, the Abbé, Hébert, and Lanty were all standing together at the head of the vessel. The poor Abbé seemed dazed, and kept dreamily fingering his rosary, and murmuring to himself. The other three consulted in a low voice.

'Were it not better to have the women here on deck?' asked Arthur.

'*Eh, non*!' sobbed Master Hébert. 'Let not my poor mistress see what is coming on her and her little ones!'

'Ah! and 'tis better if the innocent creatures must be drowned, that it should be without being insensed of it till they wake in our Lady's blessed arms,' added Lanty. 'Hark! and they are at their prayers.'

But just then Victorine rushed up from below, and throwing her arms round Lanty, cried, 'Oh! Laurent, Laurent. It is not true that it is all over with us, is it? Oh! save me! save me!'

'And if I cannot save you, mine own heart's core, we'll die together,' returned the poor fellow, holding her fast. 'It won't last long, Victorine, and the saints have a hold of my scapulary.'

He had scarcely spoken when, lifted upon a wave, the tartane dashed upon the rocks, and there was at once a horrible shivering and crashing throughout her —a frightful mingling of shrieks and yells of despair with the wild roar of the waves that poured over her. The party at the head of the vessel were conscious of clinging to something, and when the first burly-burly ceased a little they found themselves all together against the bulwark, the vessel almost on her beam ends, wedged into the rocks, their portion high and dry, but the stern, where the cabin was, entirely under water.

Victorine screamed aloud, 'My lady! my poor lady.'

'I see—I see something,' cried Arthur, who had already thrown off his coat, and in another moment he had brought up Estelle in his arms, alive, sobbing and panting. Giving her over to the steward, he made another dive, but then was lost sight of, and returned no more, nor was anything to be seen of the rest. Shut up in the cabin, Madame de Bourke, Ulysse, and the three maids must have been instantly drowned, and none of the crew were to be seen. Maître Hébert hold the little girl in his arms, glad that, though living, she was only half-conscious. Victorine, sobbing, hung heavily on Lanty, and before he could free his hands he perceived to his dismay that the Abbé, unassisted, was climbing down from the wreck upon the rock, scarcely perhaps aware of his danger.

Lanty tried to put Victorine aside, and called out, 'Your reverence, wait— Masther Phelim, wait till I come and help you.' But the girl, frantic with terror, grappled him fast, screaming to him not to let her go—and at the same moment a wave broke over the Abbé. Lanty, almost wild, was ready to leap into it after him, thinking he must be sucked back with it, but behold! he still remained clinging to the rock. Instinct seemed to serve him, for he had stuck his knife into the rock and was holding on by it. There seemed no foothold, and while Lanty was deliberating how to go to his assistance, another wave washed him off and bore him to the next rock, which was only separated from the mainland by a channel of smoother water. He tried to catch at a floating plank, but in vain; however, an oar next drifted towards him, and by it he gained the land, but only to be instantly surrounded by a mob of Cabeleyzes, who seemed to be stripping off his garments. By this time many were swimming towards the wreck; and Estelle, who had recovered breath and senses, looked over Hébert's shoulder at them. 'The savages! the infidels!' she said. 'Will they kill me? or will they try to make me renounce my faith? They shall kill me rather than make me yield.'

'Ah! yes, my dear *demoiselle*, that is right. That is the only way. It is my resolution likewise,' returned Hébert. 'God give us grace to persist.'

'My mamma said so,' repeated the child. 'Is she drowned, Maître Hébert?'

'She is happier than we are, my dear young lady.'

'And my little brother too! Ah! then I shall remember that they are only sending me to them in Paradise.'

By this time the natives were near the wreck, and Estelle, shuddering, clung closer to Hébert; but he had made up his mind what to do. 'I must commit you to these men, Mademoiselle,' he said; 'the water is rising—we shall perish if we remain here.'

'Ah! but it would not hurt so much to be drowned,' said Estelle, who had made up her mind to Blandina's chair.

'I must endeavour to save you for your father, Mademoiselle, and your poor grandmother! There! be a good child! Do not struggle.'

He had attracted the attention of some of the swimmers, and he now flung her to them. One caught her by an arm, another by a leg, and she was safely taken to the shore, where at once a shoe and a stocking were taken from her, in token of her becoming a captive; but otherwise her garments were not meddled with; in which she was happier than her uncle, whom she found crouched up on a rock, stripped almost to the skin, so that he shrank from her, when she sprang to his side amid the Babel of wild men and women, who were shouting in exultation and wonder over his big flapped hat, his *soutane* and bands, pointing at his white limbs and yellow hair—or, what amazed them even more, Estelle's light, flaxen locks, which hung soaked around her.

53

She felt a hand pulling them to see whether anything so strange actually grew on her head, and she turned round to confront them with a little gesture of defiant dignity that evidently awed them, for they kept their hands off her, and did not interfere as she stood sentry over her poor shivering uncle.

Lanty was by this time trying to drag Victorine over the rocks and through the water. The poor Parisienne was very helpless, falling, hurting herself, and screaming continually; and trebly, when a couple of natives seized upon her, and dragged her ashore, where they immediately snatched away her mantle and cap, pulled off her gold chain and cross, and tore out her earrings with howls of delight.

Lanty, struggling on, was likewise pounced upon, and bereft of his fine green and gold livery coat and waistcoat, which, though by no means his best, and stained with the sea water, were grasped with ecstasy, quarrelled over, and displayed in triumph. The steward had secured a rope by which he likewise reached the shore, only to become the prey of the savages, who instantly made prize of his watch and purse, as well as of almost all his garments. The five unfortunate survivors would fain have remained huddled together, but the natives pointing to some huts on the hillside, urged them thither by the language of shouts and blows.

'Faith and I'm not an ox,' exclaimed Lanty, as if the fellow could have understood him, 'and is it to the shambles you're driving me?'

'Best not resist! There's nothing for it but to obey them,' said the steward, 'and at least there will be shelter for the child.'

No objection was made to his lifting her in his arms, and he carried her, as the party, half-drowned, nearly starved and exhausted, stumbled on along the rocky paths which cut their feet cruelly, since their shoes had all been taken from them. Lanty gave what help he could to the Abbé and Victorine, who were both in a miserable plight, but ere long he was obliged to take his turn in carrying Estelle, whose weight had become too much for the worn out Hébert. He was alarmed to find, on transferring her, that her head sank on his shoulder as if in a sleep of exhaustion, which, however, shielded her from much terror. For, as they arrived at a cluster of five or six tents, built of clay and the branches of trees, out rushed a host of women, children, and large fierce dogs, all making as much noise as they were capable of. The dogs flew at the strange white forms, no doubt utterly new to them. Victorine was severely bitten, and Lanty, trying to rescue her, had his leg torn.

These two were driven into one hut; Estelle, who was evidently considered as the greatest prize, was taken into another and rather better one, together with the steward and the Abbé. The Moors, who had swum ashore, had probably told them that she was the Frankish Bey's daughter; for this, miserable place though it was, appeared to be the best hut in the hamlet, nor was she deprived of her clothes. A sort of bournouse or haik, of coarse texture and very dirty, was given to each of the others, and some rye cakes baked in the ashes. Poor little Estelle turned away her head at first, but Hébert, alarmed at her shivering in her wet clothes, contrived to make her swallow a little, and then took off the soaked dress, and wrapped her in the bournouse. She was by this time almost unconscious from weariness, and made no resistance to the unaccustomed hands, or the disgusting coarseness and uncleanness of her wrapper, but dropped asleep the moment he laid her down, and he applied himself to trying to dry her clothes at a little fire of sticks that had been lighted outside the open space, round which the huts stood.

The Abbé too had fallen asleep, as Hébert managed to assure poor Lanty, who rushed out of the other tent, nearly naked, and bloodstained in many places, but more concerned at his separation from his foster-brother than at anything else that had befallen him. Men, women, children, and dogs were all after him, supposing him to be trying to escape, and he was seized upon and dragged back by main force, but not before the steward had called out—

'M. l'Abbé sleeps—sleeps sound—he is not hurt! For Heaven's sake, Laurent, be quiet—do not enrage them! It is the only hope for him, as for Mademoiselle and the rest of us.'

Lanty, on hearing of the Abbé's safety, allowed himself to be taken back, making himself, however, a passive dead weight on his captor's hands.

'Arrah,' he muttered to himself, 'if ye will have me, ye shall have the trouble of me, bad luck to you. 'Tis little like ye are to the barbarous people St. Paul was thrown with; but then what right have I to expect the treatment of a holy man, the like of him? If so be, I can save that poor orphan that's left, and bring off Master Phelim safe, and save poor Victorine from being taken for some dirty spalpeen's wife, when he has half a dozen more to the fore—'tis little it matters what becomes of Lanty Callaghan; they might give him to their big brutes of dogs, and mighty lean meat they would find him!'

So came down the first night upon the captives.

CHAPTER V—CAPTIVITY

'Hold fast thy hope and Heaven will not
Forsake thee in thine hour.
Good angels will be near thee,
And evil ones will fear thee,
And Faith will give thee power.'

SOUTHEY.

The whole northern coast of Africa is inhabited by a medley of tribes, all owning a kind of subjection to the Sultan, but more in the sense of Pope than of King. The part of the coast where the tartane had been driven on the rocks was beneath Mount Araz, a spur of the Atlas, and was in the possession of the Arab tribe called Cabeleyze, which is said to mean 'the revolted.' The revolt had been from the Algerine power, which had never been able to pursue them into the fastnesses of the mountains, and they remained a wild independent race, following all those Ishmaelite traditions and customs that are innate in the blood of the Arab.

When Estelle awoke from her long sleep of exhaustion, she was conscious of a stifling atmosphere, and moreover of the crow of a cock in her immediate vicinity, then of a dog growling, and a lamb beginning to bleat. She raised herself a little, and beheld, lying on the ground around her, dark heaps with human feet protruding from them. These were interspersed with sheep, goats, dogs, and fowls, all seen by the yellow light of the rising sun which made its way in not only through the doorless aperture, but through the reeds and branches which formed the walls.

Close as the air was, she felt the chill of the morning and shivered. At the same moment she perceived poor Maître Hébert covering himself as best he could with a dirty brown garment, and bending over her with much solicitude, but making signs to make as little noise as possible, while he whispered, 'How goes it with Mademoiselle?'

'Ah,' said Estelle, recollecting herself, 'we are shipwrecked. We shall have to confess our faith! Where are the rest?'

'There is M. l'Abbé,' said Hébert, pointing to a white pair of the bare feet. 'Poor Laurent and Victorine have been carried elsewhere.'

'And mamma? And my brother?'

'Ah! Mademoiselle, give the good God thanks that he has spared them our trial.'

'Mamma! Ah, she was in the cabin when the water came in? But my brother! I had hold of his hand, he came out with me. I saw M. Arture swim away with him. Yes, Maître Hébert, indeed I did.'

Hébert had not the least hope that they could be saved, but he would not grieve the child by saying so, and his present object was to get her dressed before any one was awake to watch, and perhaps appropriate her upper garments. He was a fatherly old man, and she let him help her with her fastenings, and comb out her hair with the tiny comb in her *étui*. Indeed, *friseurs* were the rule in France, and she was not unused to male attendants at the toilette, so that she was not shocked at being left to his care.

For the rest, the child had always dwelt in an imaginary world, a curious compound of the Lives of the Saints and of Télémaque. Martyrs and heroes alike had been shipwrecked, taken captive, and tormented; and there was a certain sense of realised day-dream about her, as if she had become one of the number and must act up to her part. She asked Hébert if there were a Sainte Estelle, what was the day of the month, and if she should be placed in the Calendar if she never complained, do what these barbarians might to her. She hoped she should hold out, for she would like to be able to help all whom she loved, poor papa and all. But it was hard that mamma, who was so good, could not be a martyr too; but she was a saint in Paradise all the same, and thus Estelle made her little prayer in hope. There was no conceit or over confidence in the tone, though of course the poor child little knew what she was ready to accept; but it was a spark of the martyr's trust that gleamed in her eye, and gave her a sense of exaltation that took off the sharpest edge of grief and fear.

By this time, however, the animals were stirring, and with them the human beings who had lain down in their clothes. Peace was over; the Abbé awoke, and began to call for Laurent and his clothes and his beads; but this aroused the master of the house, who started up, and threatening with a huge stick, roared at him what must have been orders to be quiet.

Estelle indignantly flew between and cried, 'You shall not hurt my uncle.'

The commanding gesture spoke for itself; and, besides, poor Phelim cowered behind her with an air that caused a word and sign to pass round, which the captives found was equivalent to innocent or imbecile; and the Mohammedan respect and tenderness for the demented spared him all further violence or molestation, except that he was lost and miserable without the attentions of his foster-brother; and indeed the shocks he had undergone seemed to have mobbed him of much of the small degree of sense he had once possessed.

Coming into the space before the doorway, Estelle found herself the object of universal gaze and astonishment, as her long fair hair gleamed in the sunshine, every one coming to touch it, and even pull it to see if it was real. She was a good deal frightened, but too high-spirited to show it more than she could help, as the dark-skinned, bearded men crowded round with cries of wonder. The other two prisoners likewise appeared: Victorine looking wretchedly ill, and hardly able to hold up her head; Lanty creeping towards the Abbé, and trying to arrange his remnant of clothing. There was a short respite, while the Arabs, all turning eastwards, chanted their morning devotions with a solemnity that struck their captives. The scene was a fine one, if there had been any heart to admire. The huts were placed on the verge of a fine forest of chestnut and cork trees—and beyond towered up mountain peaks in every variety of dazzling colour—red and purple beneath, glowing red and gold where the snowy peaks caught the morning sun, lately broken from behind them. The slopes around were covered with rich grass, flourishing after the summer heats, and to which the herds were now betaking themselves, excepting such as were detained to be milked by the women, who came pouring out of some of the other huts in dark blue garments; and in front, still shadowed by the mountain, lay the bay, deep, beautiful, pellucid green near the land, and shut in by fantastic and picturesque rocks—some bare, some clothed with splendid foliage, winter though it was—while beyond lay the exquisite blue stretching to the horizon. Little recked the poor prisoners of the scene so fair; they only saw the remnant of the wreck below, the sea that parted them from hope, the savage rocks behind, the barbarous people around, the squalor and dirt of the adowara, as the hamlet was called.

Comparatively, the Moor who had swum ashore to reconnoitre seemed like a friend when he came forward and saluted Estelle and the Abbé respectfully. Moreover the *lingua Franca* Lanty had picked up established a very imperfect double system of interpretation by the help of many gestures. This was Lanty's explanation to the rest: in French, of course, but, like all his speech, Irish-English in construction.

'This Moor, Hassan, wants to stand our friend in his own fashion, but he says they care not the value of an empty mussel-shell for the French, and no more for the Dey of Algiers than I do for the Elector of Hanover. He has told them that M. l'Abbé and Mademoiselle are brother and daughter to a great Bey— but it is little they care for that. Holy Virgin, they took Mademoiselle for a boy! That is why they are gazing at her so impudently. Would that I could give them a taste of my cane! Do you see those broken walls, and a bit of a castle on yonder headland jutting out into the sea? They are bidding Hassan say that the French built that, and garrisoned it with the help of the Dey; but there fell out a war, and these fellows, or their fathers, surprised it, sacked it, and carried off four hundred prisoners into slavery. Holy Mother defend us! Here are all the rogues coming to see what they will do with us!'

For the open space in front of the huts, whence all the animals had now been driven, was becoming thronged with figures with the haik laid over their heads, spear or blunderbuss in hand, fine bearing, and sometimes truculent, though handsome, browse countenances. They gazed at the captives, and uttered what sounded like loud hurrahs or shouts; but after listening to Hassan, Lanty turned round trembling. 'The miserables! Some are for sacrificing us outright on the spot, but this decent man declares that he will make them sensible that their prophet was not out-and-out as bad as that. Never you fear, Mademoiselle.'

'I am not afraid,' said Estelle, drawing up her head. 'We shall be martyrs.'

Lanty was engaged in listening to a moan from his foster-brother for food, and Hébert joined in observing that they might as well be sacrificed as starved to death; whereupon the Irishman's words and gesticulations induced the Moor to make representations which resulted in some dry pieces of *samh* cake, a few dates, and a gourd of water being brought by one of the women; a scanty amount for the number, even though poor Victorine was too ill to touch anything but the water; while the Abbé seemed unable to understand that the servants durst not demand anything better, and devoured her share and a quarter of Lanty's as well as his own. Meantime the Cabeleyzes had all ranged themselves in rows, cross-legged on the ground, opposite to the five unfortunate captives, to sit in judgment on them. As they kept together in one group, happily in the shade of a hut, Victorine, too faint and sick fully to know what was going on, lay with her head on the lap of her young mistress, who sat with her bright and strangely fearless eyes confronting the wild figures opposite.

Her uncle, frightened, though not comprehending the extent of his danger, crouched behind Lanty, who with Hébert stood somewhat in advance, the would-be guardians of the more helpless ones.

There was an immense amount of deafening shrieking and gesticulating among the Arabs. Hassan was responding, and finally turned to Lanty, when the anxious watchers could perceive signs as if of paying down coin made interrogatively. 'Promise them anything, everything,' cried Hébert; 'M. le Comte would give his last sou—so would Madame la Marquise—to save Mademoiselle.'

'I have told him so,' said Laurence presently; 'I bade him let them know it is little they can make of us, specially now they have stripped us as bare as themselves, the rascals! but that their fortunes would be made—and little they would know what to do with them—if they would only send M. l'Abbé and Mademoiselle to Algiers safe and sound. There! he is trying to incense them. Never fear, Master Phelim, dear, there never was a rogue yet, black or white, or the colour of poor Madame's frothed chocolate, who did not love gold better than blood, unless indeed 'twas for the sweet morsel of revenge; and these, for all their rolling eyes and screeching tongues, have not the ghost of a quarrel with us.'

'My beads, my breviary,' sighed the Abbé. 'Get them for me, Lanty.'

'I wish they would end it quickly,' said Estelle. 'My head aches so, and I want to be with mamma. Poor Victorine! yours is worse,' she added, and soaked her handkerchief in the few drops of water left in the gourd to lay it on the maid's forehead.

The howling and shrieking betokened consultation, but was suddenly interrupted by some half-grown lads, who came running in with their hands full of what Lanty recognised to his horror as garments worn by his mistress and fellow-servants, also a big kettle and a handspike. They pointed down to the sea, and with yells of haste and exultation all the wild conclave started up to snatch, handle, and examine, then began rushing headlong to the beach. Hassan's explanations were scarcely needed to show that they were about to ransack the ship, and he evidently took credit to himself for having induced them to spare the prisoners in case their assistance should be requisite to gain full possession of the plunder.

Estelle and Victorine were committed to the charge of a forbidding-looking old hag, the mother of the sheyk of the party; the Abbé was allowed to stray about as he pleased, but the two men were driven to the shore by the eloquence of the club. Victorine revived enough for a burst of tears and a sobbing cry, 'Oh, they will be killed! We shall never see them again!'

'No,' said Estelle, with her quiet yet childlike resolution, 'they are not going to kill any of us yet. They said so. You are so tired, poor Victorine! Now all the hubbub is over, suppose you lie still and sleep. My uncle,' as he roamed round her, mourning for his rosary, 'I am afraid your beads are lost; but see here, these little round seeds, I can pierce them if you will gather some more for me, and make you another set. See, these will be the Aves, and here are shells in the grass for the Paters.'

The long fibre of grass served for the string, and the sight of the Giaour girl's employment brought round her all the female population who had not repaired to the coast. Her first rosary was torn from her to adorn an almost naked baby; but the Abbé began to whimper, and to her surprise the mother restored it to him. She then made signs that she would construct another necklace for the child, and she was rewarded by a gourd being brought to her full of milk, which she was able to share with her two companions, and which did something to revive poor Victorine. Estelle was kept threading these necklaces and bracelets all the wakeful hours of the day—for every one fell asleep about noon—though still so jealous a watch was kept on her that she was hardly allowed to shift her position so as to get out of the sun, which even at that season was distressingly scorching in the middle of the day.

Parties were continually coming up from the beach laden with spoils of all kinds from the wreck, Lanty, Hébert, and a couple of negroes being driven up repeatedly, so heavily burthened as to be almost bent double. All was thrown down in a heap at the other end of the adowara, and the old sheyk kept guard over it, allowing no one to touch it. This went on till darkness was coming on, when, while the cattle were being collected for the night, the prisoners were allowed an interval, in which Hébert and Lanty told how the natives, swimming like ducks, had torn everything out of the wreck: all the bales and boxes that poor Maître Hébert had secured with so much care, and many of which he was now forced himself to open for the pleasure of these barbarians.

That, however, was not the worst. Hébert concealed from his little lady what Lanty did not spare Victorine. 'And there—enough to melt the heart of a stone—there lay on the beach poor Madame la Comtesse, and all the three. Good was it for you, Victorine, my jewel, that you were not in the cabin with them.'

'I know not,' said the dejected Victorine; 'they are better off than we?'

'You would not say so, if you had seen what I have,' said Lanty, shuddering. 'The dogs!—they cut off Madame's poor white fingers to get at her rings, and not with knives either, lest her blessed flesh should defile them, they said, and her poor face was an angel's all the time. Nay, nor that was not the worst. The villainous boys, what must they do but pelt the poor swollen bodies with stones! Ay, well you may scream, Victorine. We went down on our knees, Maître Hébert and I, to pray they might let us give them burial, but they mocked us, and bade Hassan say they never bury dogs. I went round the steeper path, for all the load at my back, or I should have been flying at the throats of the cowardly vultures, and then what would have become of M. l'Abbé?'

Victorine trembled and wept bitterly for her companions, and then asked if Lanty had seen the corpse of the little Chevalier.

'Not a sight of him or M. Arthur either,' returned Lanty; 'only the ugly face of the old Turk captain and another of his crew, and them they buried decently, being Moslem hounds like themselves; while my poor lady that is a saint in heaven—' and he, too, shed tears of hot grief and indignation, recovering enough to warn Victorine by no means to let the poor young girl know of this additional horror.

There was little opportunity, for they had been appropriated by different masters: Estelle, the Abbé, and Hébert to the sheyk, or headman of the clan; and Lanty and Victorine to a big, strong, fierce-looking fellow, of inferior degree but greater might.

This time Estelle was to be kept for the night among the sheyk's women, who, though too unsophisticated to veil their faces, had a part of the hut closed off with a screen of reeds, but quite as bare as the outside. Hébert, who could not endure to think of her sleeping on the ground, and saw a large heap of grass or straw provided for a little brown cow, endeavoured to take an armful for her. Unluckily it belonged to Lanty's master, Eyoub, who instantly flew at him in a fury, dragged him to a log of wood, caught up an axe, and had not Estelle's screams brought up the sheyk, with Hassan and one or two other men, the poor Maître d'Hôtel's head would have been off. There was a sharp altercation between the sheyk and Eyoub, while Estelle held the faithful servant's hand, saying, 'You did it for me! Oh, Hébert, do not make them angry again. It would be beautiful to die for one's faith, but not for a handful of hay.'

'Ah! my dear *demoiselle*, what would my poor ladies say to see you sleeping on the bare ground in a filthy hut?'

'I slept well last night,' returned Estelle; 'indeed, I do not mind! It is only the more like the dungeon at Lyon, you know! And I pray you, Hébert, do not get yourself killed for nothing too soon, or else we shall not all stand out and confess together, like St. Blandina and St. Ponticus and St Epagathius.'

'Alas, the dear child! The long names run off her tongue as glibly as ever,' sighed Hébert, who, though determined not to forsake his faith, by no means partook her enthusiasm for martyrdom. Hassan, however, having explained what the purpose had been, Hébert was pardoned, though the sheyk scornfully observed that what was good enough for the daughters of a Hadji was good enough for the unclean child of the Frankish infidels.

The hay might perhaps have spared a little stiffness, but it would not have ameliorated the chief annoyances—the closeness, the dirt, and the vermin. It was well that it was winter, or the first of these would have been far worse, and, fortunately for Estelle, she was one of those whom suffocating air rather lulls than rouses.

Eyoub's hovel did not rejoice in the refinement of a partition, but his family, together with their animals, lay on the rocky floor as best they might; and Victorine's fever came on again, so that she lay in great misery, greeted by a growl from a great white dog whenever she tried to relieve her restless aching limbs by the slightest movement, or to reach one of the gourds of water laid near the sleepers, like Saul's cruse at his pillow.

Towards morning, however, Lanty, who had been sitting with his back against the wall, awoke from the sleep well earned by acting as a beast of burthen. The dog growled a little, but Lanty—though his leg still showed its teeth-marks—had made friends with it, and his hand on its head quieted it directly, so that he was able cautiously to hand a gourd to Victorine. The Arabs were heavy sleepers, and the two were able to talk under their breath; as, in reply to a kind word from Lanty, poor Victorine moaned her envy of the fate of Rosette and Babette; and he, with something of their little mistress's spirit, declared that he had no doubt but that 'one way or the other they should be out of it: either get safe home, or be blessed martyrs, without even a taste of purgatory.'

'Ah! but there's worse for me,' sighed Victorine. 'This demon brought another to stare in my face—I know he wants to make me his wife! Kill me first, Laurent.'

'It is I that would rather espouse you, my jewel,' returned a tender whisper.

'How can you talk of such things at such a moment?'

''Tis a pity M. l'Abbé is not a priest,' sighed Lanty. 'But, you know, Victorine, who is the boy you always meant to take.'

'You need not be so sure of that,' she said, the coy coquetry not quite extinct.

'Come, as you said, it is no time for fooling. Give me your word and troth to be my wife so soon as we have the good luck to come by a Christian priest by our Lady's help, and I'll outface them all—were it Mohammed the Prophet himself, that you are my espoused and betrothed, and woe to him that puts a finger on you.'

'You would only get yourself killed.'

'And would not I be proud to be killed for your sake? Besides, I'll show them cause not to kill me if I have the chance. Trust me, Victorine, my darling—it is but a chance among these murdering villains, but it is the only one; and, sure, if you pretended to turn the back of your hand to me when there were plenty of Christian men to compliment you, yet you would rather have poor Lanty than a thundering rogue of a pagan Mohammedan.'

'I hope I shall die,' sighed poor Victorine faintly. 'It will only be your death!'

'That is my affair,' responded Lanty. 'Come, here's daylight coming in; reach me your hand before this *canaille* wakes, and here's this good beast of a dog, and yonder grave old goat with a face like Père Michel's for our witnesses— and by good luck, here's a bit of gilt wire off my shoulder-knot that I've made into a couple of rings while I've been speaking.'

The strange betrothal had barely taken place before there was a stir, and what was no doubt a yelling imprecation on the 'dog Giaours' for the noise they made.

The morning began as before, with the exception that Estelle had established a certain understanding with a little chocolate-coloured cupid of a boy of the size of her brother, and his lesser sister, by letting them stroke her hair, and showing them the mysteries of cat's cradle. They shared their gourd of goat's-milk with her, but would not let her give any to her companions. However, the Abbé had only to hold out his hand to be fed, and the others were far too anxious to care much about their food.

A much larger number of Cabeleyzes came streaming into the forum of the adowara, and the prisoners were all again placed in a row, while the new-comers passed before them, staring hard, and manifestly making personal remarks which perhaps it was well that they did not understand. The sheyk and Eyoub evidently regarded them as private property, stood in front, and permitted nobody to handle them, which was so far a comfort.

Then followed a sort of council, with much gesticulation, in which Hassan took his share. Then, followed by the sheyk, Eyoub, and some other headmen, he advanced, and demanded that the captives should become true believers. This was eked out with gestures betokening that thus they would be free, in that case; while, if they refused, the sword and the smouldering flame were pointed to, while the whole host loudly shouted 'Islam!'

Victorine trembled, sobbed, tried to hide herself; but Estelle stood up, her young face lighted up, her dark eyes gleaming, as if she were realising a daydream, as she shook her head, cried out to Lanty, 'Tell him, No—never!' and held to her breast a little cross of sticks that she had been forming to complete her uncle's rosary. Her gesture was understood. A man better clad than the rest, with a turban and a broad crimson sash, rushed up to her, seized her by the hair, and waved his scimitar over her head. The child felt herself close to her mother. She looked up in his face with radiant eyes and a smile on her lips. It absolutely daunted the fellow: his arm dropped, and he gazed at her like some supernatural creature; and the sheyk, enraged at the interference with his property, darted forth to defend it, and there was a general wrangling.

Seconded by their interpreter, Hassan, who knew that the Koran did not prescribe the destruction of Christians, Hébert and Lanty endeavoured to show that their conversion was out of the question, and that their slaughter would only be the loss of an exceedingly valuable ransom, which would be paid if they were handed over safe and sound and in good condition.

There was no knowing what was the effect of this, for the council again ended in a rush to secure the remaining pillage of the wreck. Hébert and Lanty dreaded what they might see, but to their great relief those poor remains had disappeared. They shuddered as they remembered the hyenas' laughs and the jackals' howls they had heard at nightfall; but though they hoped that the sea

66

had been merciful, they could even have been grateful to the animals that had spared them the sight of conscious insults.

The wreck was finally cleared, and among the fragments were found several portions of books. These the Arabs disregarded, being too ignorant even to read their own Koran, and yet aware of the Mohammedan scruple which forbids the destruction of any scrap of paper lest it should bear the name of Allah. Lanty secured the greater part of the Abbé's breviary, and a good many pages of Estelle's beloved Télémaque; while the steward gained possession of his writing case, and was permitted to retain it when the Cabeleyzes, glutted with plunder, had ascertained that it contained nothing of value to them.

After everything had been dragged up to the adowara, there ensued a sort of auction or division of the plunder. Poor Maître Hébert was doomed to see the boxes and bales he had so diligently watched broken open by these barbarians,—nay, he had to assist in their own dissection when the secrets were too much for the Arabs. There was the King of Spain's portrait rent from its costly setting and stamped upon as an idolatrous image. The miniature of the Count, worn by the poor lady, had previously shared the same fate, but that happily was out of sight and knowledge. Here was the splendid plate, presented by crowned heads, howled over by savages ignorant of its use. The silver they seemed to value; but there were three precious gold cups which the salt water had discoloured, so that they were taken for copper and sold for a very small price to a Jew, who somehow was attracted to the scene, 'like a raven to the slaughter,' said Lanty.

This man likewise secured some of the poor lady's store of rich dresses, but a good many more were appropriated to make sashes for the men, and the smaller articles, including stockings, were wound turban fashion round the children's heads.

Lanty could not help observing, 'And if the saints are merciful to us, and get us out of this, we shall have stories to tell that will last our lives!' as he watched the solemn old chief smelling to the perfumes, swallowing the rouge as splendid medicine, and finally fingering a snuff-box, while half a dozen more crowded round to assist in the opening, and in another moment sneezing, weeping, tingling, dancing frantically about, vituperating the Christian's magic.

This gave Lanty an idea. A little round box lay near, which, as he remembered, contained a Jack-in-the-box, or Polichinelle, which the poor little Chevalier had bought at the fair at Tarascon. This he contrived to secrete and hand to Victorine. 'Keep the secret,' he said, 'and you will find your best guardian in that bit of a box.' And when that very evening an Arab showed some intentions of adding her to his harem, Victorine bethought herself of the box, and unhooked in desperation. Up sprang Punch, long-nosed and fur-capped, right in the bearded face.

Back the man almost fell; 'Shaitan, Shaitan!' was the cry, as the inhabitants tumbled pell-mell out of the hovel, and Victorine and Punch remained masters of the situation.

She heard Lanty haranguing in broken Arabic and *lingua Franca*, and presently he came in, shaking with suppressed laughter. 'If ever we get home,' said he, 'we'll make a pilgrimage to Tarascon! Blessings on good St. Martha that put that sweet little imp in my way! The rogues think he is the very genie that the fisherman let out of the bottle in Mademoiselle's book of the Thousand and One Nights, and thought to see him towering over the whole place. And a fine figure he would be with his hook nose and long beard. They sent me to beg you fairly to put up your little Shaitan again. I told them that Shaitan, as they call him, is always in it when there's meddling between an espoused pair—which is as true as though the Holy Father at Rome had said it—and as long as they were civil, Shaitan would rest; but if they durst molest you, there was no saying where he would be, if once you had to let him out! To think of the virtue of that ugly face and bit of a coil of wire!'

Meantime Hébert, having ascertained that both the Jew and Hassan were going away, the one to Constantina, the other to Algiers, wrote, and so did Estelle, to the Consul at Algiers, explaining their position and entreating to be ransomed. Though only nine years old, Estelle could write a very fair letter, and the amazement of the Arabs was unbounded that any female creature should wield a pen. Marabouts and merchants were known to read the Koran, but if one of the goats had begun to write, their wonder could hardly have been greater; and such crowds came to witness the extraordinary operation that she could scarcely breathe or see.

It seemed to establish her in their estimation as a sort of supernatural being, for she was always treated with more consideration than the rest of the captives, never deprived of the clothes she wore, and allowed to appropriate a few of the toilette necessaries that were quite incomprehensible to those around her.

She learnt the names for bread, chestnuts, dates, milk, and water, and these were never denied to her; and her little ingenuities in nursery games won the goodwill of the women and children around her, though others used to come and make ugly faces at her, and cry out at her as an unclean thing. The Abbé was allowed to wander about at will, and keep his Hours, with Estelle to make the responses, and sometimes Hébert. He was the only one that might visit the other two captives; Lanty was kept hard at work over the crop of chestnuts that the clan had come down from their mountains to gather in; and poor Victorine, who was consumed by a low fever, and almost too weak to move, lay all day in the dreary and dirty hut, expecting, but dreading death.

Some days later there was great excitement, shouting, and rage. It proved that the Bey of Constantina had sent to demand the party, threatening to send an armed force to compel their surrender; but, alas! the hope of a return to comparative civilisation was instantly quashed, for the sheyk showed himself furious. He and Eyoub stood brandishing their scimitars, and with eyes flashing like a panther's in the dark, declaring that they were free, no subjects of the Dey nor the Bey either; and that they would shed the blood of every one of the captives rather than yield them to the dogs and sons of dogs at Constantina.

This embassy only increased the jealousy with which the prisoners were guarded. None of them were allowed to stir without a man with a halbert, and they had the greatest difficulty in entrusting a third letter to the Moor in command of the party. Indeed, it was only managed by Estelle's coaxing of the little Abou Daoud, who was growing devoted to her, and would do anything for the reward of hearing her sing life *Malbrook s'en va-t'-n guerre.*

It might have been in consequence of this threat of the Bey, much as they affected to despise it, that the Cabeleyzes prepared to return to the heights of Mount Araz, whence they had only descended during the autumn to find fresh pasture for their cattle, and to collect dates and chestnuts from the forest.

'Alas!' said Hubert, 'this is worse than ever. As long as we were near the sea, I had hope, but now all trace of us will be lost, even if the Consul should send after us.'

'Never fear, Maître Hubert,' said Estelle; 'you know Télémaque was a prisoner and tamed the wild peasants in Egypt.'

'Ah! the poor demoiselle, she always seems as if she were acting a comedy.'

This was happily true. Estelle seemed to be in a curious manner borne through the dangers and discomforts of her surroundings by a strange dreamy sense of living up to her part, sometimes as a possible martyr, sometimes as a figure in the mythological or Arcadian romance that had filtered into her nursery.

CHAPTER VI—A MOORISH VILLAGE

'Our laws and our worship on thee thou shalt take,
And this shalt thou first do for Zulema's sake.'

SCOTT.

When Arthur Hope dashed back from the party on the prow of the wrecked tartane in search of little Ulysse, he succeeded in grasping the child, but at the same moment a huge breaker washed him off the slipperily-sloping deck, and after a scarce conscious struggle he found himself, still retaining his clutch of the boy, in the trough between it and another. He was happily an expert swimmer, and holding the little fellow's clothes in his teeth, he was able to avoid the dash, and to rise on another wave. Then he perceived that he was no longer near the vessel, but had been carried out to some little distance, and his efforts only succeeded in keeping afloat, not in approaching the shore. Happily a plank drifted so near him that he was able to seize it and throw himself across it, thus obtaining some support, and being able to raise the child farther above the water.

At the same time he became convinced that a strong current, probably from a river or stream, was carrying him out to sea, away from the bay. He saw the black heads of two or three of the Moorish crew likewise floating on spars, and yielding themselves to the stream, and this made him better satisfied to follow their example. It was a sort of rest, and gave him time to recover from the first exhaustion to convince himself that the little boy was not dead, and to lash him to the plank with a handkerchief.

By and by—he knew not how soon—calls and shouts passed between the Moors; only two seemed to survive, and they no longer obeyed the direction of the current, but turned resolutely towards the land, where Arthur dimly saw a green valley opening towards the sea. This was a much severer effort, but by this time immediate self-preservation had become the only thought, and happily both wind and the very slight tide were favourable, so that, just as the sun sank beneath the western waves, Arthur felt foothold on a sloping beach of white sand, even as his powers became exhausted. He struggled up out of reach of the sea, and then sank down, exhausted and unconscious.

His first impression was of cries and shrieks round him, as he gasped and panted, then saw as in a dream forms flitting round him, and then—feeling for the child and missing him—he raised himself in consternation, and the movement was greeted by fresh unintelligible exclamations, while a not unkindly hand lifted him up. It belonged to a man in a sort of loose white garment and drawers, with a thin dark-bearded face; and Arthur, recollecting that the Spanish word *niño* passed current for child in *lingua Franca*, uttered it with an accent of despairing anxiety. He was answered with a volley of words that he only understood to be in a consoling tone, and the speaker pointed inland. Various persons, among whom Arthur saw his recent shipmates, seemed to be going in that direction, and he obeyed his guide, though scarcely able to move from exhaustion and cold, the garments he had retained clinging about him. Some one, however, ran down towards him with a vessel containing a draught of sour milk. This revived him enough to see clearly and follow his guides. After walking a distance, which appeared to him most laborious, he found himself entering a sort of village, and was ushered through a courtyard into a kind of room. In the centre a fire was burning; several figures were busy round it, and in another moment he perceived that they were rubbing, chafing, and otherwise restoring his little companion.

Indeed Ulysse had just recovered enough to be terribly frightened, and as his friend's voice answered his screams, he sprang from the kind brown hands, and, darting on Arthur, clung to him with face hidden on his shoulder. The women who had been attending to him fell back as the white stranger entered, and almost instantly dry clothes were brought, and while Arthur was warming himself and putting them on, a little table about a foot high was set, the contents of a cauldron of a kind of soup which had been suspended over the fire were poured into a large round green crock, and in which all were expected to dip their spoons and fingers. Little Ulysse was exceedingly amazed, and observed that *ces gens* were not *bien élevés* to eat out of the dish; but he was too hungry to make any objection to being fed with the wooden spoon that had been handed to Arthur; and when the warm soup, and the meat floating in it, had refreshed them, signs were made to them to lie down on a mat within an open door, and both were worn out enough to sleep soundly.

It was daylight when Arthur was awakened by poor little Ulysse sitting up and crying out for his *bonne*, his mother, and sister, 'Oh! take me to them,' he cried; 'I do not like this dark place.'

For dark the room was, being windowless, though the golden sunlight could be seen beyond the open doorway, which was under a sort of cloister or verandah overhung by some climbing plant. Arthur, collecting himself, reminded the child how the waves had borne them away from the rest, with earnest soothing promises of care, and endeavouring to get back to the rest. 'Say your prayers that God will take care of you and bring you back to your sister,' Arthur added, for he did not think it possible that the child's mother should have been saved from the waves; and his heart throbbed at thoughts of his promise to the poor lady.

'But I want my *bonne*,' sighed Ulysse; 'I want my clothes. This is an ugly *robe de nuit*, and there is no bed.'

'Perhaps we can find your clothes,' said Arthur. 'They were too wet to be kept on last night.'

So they emerged into the court, which had a kind of farmyard appearance; women with rows of coins hanging over their brows were milking cows and goats, and there was a continuous confusion of sound of their voices, and the lowing and bleating of cattle. At the appearance of Arthur and the boy, there was a general shout, and people seemed to throng in to gaze at them, the men handsome, stately, and bearded, with white full drawers, and a bournouse laid so as first to form a flat hood over the head, and then belted in at the waist, with a more or less handsome sash, into which were stuck a spoon and knife, and in some cases one or two pistols. They did not seem ill-disposed, though their language was perfectly incomprehensible. Ulysse's clothes were lying dried by the hearth and no objection was made to his resuming them. Arthur made gestures of washing or bathing, and was conducted outside the court, to a little stream of pure water descending rapidly to the sea. It was so cold that Ulysse screamed at the touch, as Arthur, with more spectators than he could have desired, did his best to perform their toilettes. He had divested himself of most of his own garments for the convenience of swimming, but his pockets were left and a comb in them; and though poor Mademoiselle Julienne would have been shocked at the result of his efforts, and the little silken laced suit was sadly tarnished with sea water, Ulysse became such an astonishing sight that the children danced round him, the women screamed with wonder, and the men said 'Mashallah!' The young Scotsman's height was perhaps equally amazing, for he saw them pointing up to his head as if measuring his stature.

He saw that he was in a village of low houses, with walls of unhewn stone, enclosing yards, and set in the midst of fruit-trees and gardens. Though so far on in the autumn there was a rich luxuriant appearance; roots and fruits, corn and flax, were laid out to dry, and girls and boys were driving the cattle out to pasture. He could not doubt that he had landed among a settled and not utterly uncivilised people, but he was too spent and weary to exert himself, or even to care for much beyond present safety; and had no sooner returned to his former quarters, and shared with Ulysse a bowl of curds, than they both feel asleep again in the shade of the gourd plant trained on a trellised roof over the wall.

When he next awoke, Ulysse was very happily at play with some little brown children, as if the sports of childhood defied the curse of Babel, and a sailor from the tartane was being greeted by the master of the house. Arthur hoped that some communication would now be possible, but, unfortunately, the man knew very little of the *lingua Franca* of the Mediterranean, and Arthur knew still less. However, he made out that he was the only one of the shipwrecked crew who had managed to reach the land, and that this was a village of Moors —settled agricultural Moors, not Arabs, good Moslems—who would do him no harm. This, and he pointed to a fine-looking elderly man, was the sheyk of the village, Abou Ben Zegri, and if the young Giaours would conform to the true faith all would be *salem* with them. Arthur shook his head, and tried by word and sign to indicate his anxiety for the rest of his companions. The sailor threw up his hands, and pointed towards the sea, to show that he believed them to be all lost; but Arthur insisted that five—marking them off on his fingers—were on *gebal*, a rock, and emphatically indicated his desire of reaching them. The Moor returned the word 'Cabeleyzes,' with gestures signifying throat-cutting and slavery, also that these present hosts regarded them as banditti. How far off they were it was not possible to make out, for of course Arthur's own sensations were no guide; but he knew that the wreck had taken place early in the afternoon, and that he had come on shore in the dusk, which was then at about five o'clock. There was certainly a promontory, made by the ridge of a hill, and also a river between him and any survivors there might be.

This was all that he could gather, and he was not sure of even thus much, but he was still too much wearied and battered for any exertion of thought or even anxiety. Three days' tempest in a cockle-shell of a ship, and then three hours' tossing on a plank, had left him little but the desire of repose, and the Moors were merciful and let him alone. It was a beautiful place—that he already knew. A Scot, and used to the sea-coast, his eye felt at home as it ranged to the grand heights in the dim distance, with winter caps of snow, and shaded in the most gorgeous tints of colouring forests beneath, slopes covered with the exquisite green of young wheat. Autumn though it was, the orange-trees, laden with fruit, the cork-trees, ilexes, and fan-palms, gave plenty of greenery, shading the gardens with prickly pear hedges; and though many of the fruit-trees had lost their leaves, fig, peach, and olive, and mulberry, caper plants, vines with foliage of every tint of red and purple, which were trained over the trellised courts of the houses, made everything have a look of rural plenty and peace, most unlike all that Arthur had ever heard or imagined of the Moors, who, as he owned to himself, were certainly not all savage pirates and slave-drivers. The whole within was surrounded by a stone wall, with a deep horse-shoe-arched gateway, the fields and pastures lying beyond with some more slightly-walled enclosures meant for the protection of the flocks and herds at night.

He saw various arts going on. One man was working in iron over a little charcoal fire, with a boy to blow up his bellows, and several more were busied over some pottery, while the women alternated their grinding between two mill stones, and other domestic cares, with spinning, weaving, and beautiful embroidery. To Arthur, who looked on, with no one to speak to except little Ulysse, it was strangely like seeing the life of the Israelites in the Old Testament when they dwelt under their own vines and fig-trees—like reading a chapter in the Bible, as he said to himself, as again and again he saw some allusion to Eastern customs illustrated. He was still more struck— when, after the various herds of kine, sheep, and goats, with one camel, several asses, and a few slender-limbed Barbary horses had been driven in for the night—by the sight of the population, as the sun sank behind the mountains, all suspending whatever they were about, spreading their prayer carpets, turning eastwards, performing their ablutions, and uttering their brief prayer with one voice so devoutly that he was almost struck with awe.

'Are they saying their prayers?' whispered Ulysse, startled by the instant change in his play-fellows, and as Arthur acquiesced, 'Then they are good.'

'If it were the true faith,' said Arthur, thinking of the wide difference between this little fellow and Estelle; but though not two years younger, Ulysse was far more childish than his sister, and when she was no longer present to lead him with her enthusiasm, sank at once to his own level. He opened wide his eyes at Arthur's reply, and said, 'I do not see their idols.'

'They have none,' said Arthur, who could not help thinking that Ulysse might look nearer home for idols—but chiefly concerned at the moment to keep the child quiet, lest he should bring danger on them by interruption.

They were sitting in the embowered porch of the sheyk's court when, a few seconds after the villagers had risen up from their prayer, they saw a figure enter at the village gateway, and the sheyk rise and go forward. There were low bending in salutation, hands placed on the breast, then kisses exchanged, after which the Sheyk Abou Ben Zegri went out with the stranger, and great excitement and pleasure seemed to prevail among the villagers, especially the women. Arthur heard the word 'Yusuf' often repeated, and by the time darkness had fallen on the village, the sheyk ushered the guest into his court, bringing with him a donkey with some especially precious load—which was removed; after which the supper was served as before in the large low apartment, with a handsomely tiled floor, and an opening in the roof for the issue of the smoke from the fire, which became agreeable in the evening at this season. Before supper, however, the stranger's feet and hands were washed by a black slave in Eastern fashion; and then all, as before, sat on mats or cushions round the central bowl, each being furnished with a spoon and thin flat soft piece of bread to dip into the mess of stewed kid, flakes of which might be extracted with the fingers.

The women, who had fastened a piece of linen across their faces, ran about and waited on the guests, who included three or four of the principal men of the village, as well as the stranger, who, as Arthur observed, was not of the uniform brown of the rest, but had some colour in his cheeks, light eyes, and a ruddy beard, and also was of a larger frame than these Moors, who, though graceful, lithe, and exceedingly stately and dignified, hardly reached above young Hope's own shoulder. Conversation was going on all the time, and Arthur soon perceived that he was the subject of it. As soon as the meal was over, the new-comer addressed him, to his great joy, in French. It was the worst French imaginable—perhaps more correctly *lingua Franca*, with a French instead of an Arabic foundation, but it was more comprehensible than that of the Moorish sailor, and bore some relation to a civilised language; besides which there was something indescribably familiar in the tone of voice, although Arthur's good French often missed of being comprehended.

'Son of a great man? Ambassador, French!' The greatness seemed impressed, but whether ambassador was understood was another thing, though it was accepted as relating to the boy.

'Secretary to the Ambassador' seemed to be an equal problem. The man shook his head, but he took in better the story of the wreck, though, like the sailor, he shook his head over the chance of there being any survivors, and utterly negatived the idea of joining them. The great point that Arthur tried to convey was that there would be a very considerable ransom if the child could be conveyed to Algiers, and he endeavoured to persuade the stranger, who was evidently a sort of travelling merchant, and, as he began to suspect, a renegade, to convey them thither; but he only got shakes of the head as answers, and something to the effect that they were a good deal out of the Dey's reach in those parts, together with what he feared was an intimation that they were altogether in the power of Sheyk Abou Ben Zegri.

They were interrupted by a servant of the merchant, who came to bring him some message as well as a pipe and tobacco. The pipe was carried by a negro boy, at sight of whom Ulysse gave a cry of ecstasy, 'Juba! Juba! Grandmother's Juba! Why do not you speak to me?' as the little black, no bigger than Ulysse himself, grinned with all his white teeth, quite uncomprehending.

'Ah! my poor laddie,' exclaimed Arthur in his native tongue, which he often used with the boy, 'it is only another negro. You are far enough from home.'

The words had an astonishing effect on the merchant. He turned round with the exclamation, 'Ye'll be frae Scotland!'

'And so are you!' cried Arthur, holding out his hand.

'Tak tent, tak tent,' said the merchant hastily, yet with a certain hesitation, as though speaking a long unfamiliar tongue. 'The loons might jalouse our being overfriendly thegither.'

Then he returned to the sheyk, to whom he seemed to be making explanations, and presenting some of his tobacco, which probably was of a superior quality in preparation to what was grown in the village. They solemnly smoked together and conversed, while Arthur watched them anxiously, relieved that he had found an interpreter, but very doubtful whether a renegade could be a friend, even though he were indeed a fellow-countryman.

It was not till several pipes had been consumed, and the village worthies had, with considerable ceremony, taken leave, that the merchant again spoke to Arthur. 'I'll see ye the morn; I hae tell'd the sheyk we are frae the same parts. Maybe I can serve you, if ye ken what's for your guid, but I canna say mair the noo.'

The sheyk escorted him out of the court, for he slept in one of the two striped horse-hair tents, which had been spread within the enclosures belonging to the village, around which were tethered the mules and asses that carried his wares. Arthur meanwhile arranged his little charge for the night.

He felt that among these enemies to their faith he must do what was in his power to keep up that of the child, and not allow his prayers to be neglected; but not being able to repeat the Latin forms, and thinking them unprofitable to the boy himself, he prompted the saying of the Creed and Lord's Prayer in English, and caused them to be repeated after him, though very sleepily and imperfectly.

All the men of the establishment seemed to take their night's rest on a mat, wrapped in a bournouse, wherever they chanced to find themselves, provided it was under shelter; the women in some *penetralia* beyond a doorway, though they were not otherwise secluded, and only partially veiled their faces at sight of a stranger. Arthur had by this time made out that the sheyk, who was a very handsome man over middle-age, seemed to have two wives; one probably of his own age, and though withered up into a brown old mummy, evidently the ruler at home, wearing the most ornaments, and issuing her orders in a shrill, cracked tone. There was a much younger and handsome one, the mother apparently of two or three little girls from ten or twelve years old to five, and there was a mere girl, with beautiful melancholy gazelle-like eyes, and a baby in her arms. She wore no ornaments, but did not seem to be classed with the slaves who ran about at the commands of the elder dame.

However, his own position was a matter of much more anxious care, although he had more hope of discovering what it really was.

He had, however, to be patient. The sunrise orisons were no sooner paid than there was a continual resort to the tent of the merchant, who was found sitting there calmly smoking his long pipe, and ready to offer the like, also a cup of coffee, to all who came to traffic with him. He seemed to have a miscellaneous stock of coffee, tobacco, pipes, preparations of sugar, ornaments in gold and silver, jewellery, charms, pistols, and a host of other articles in stock, and to be ready to purchase or barter these for the wax, embroidered handkerchiefs, yarn, and other productions and manufactures of the place. Not a single purchase could be made on either side without a tremendous haggling, shouting, and gesticulating, as if the parties were on the verge of coming to blows; whereas all was in good fellowship, and a pleasing excitement and diversion where time was of no value to anybody. Arthur began to despair of ever gaining attention. He was allowed to wander about as he pleased within the village gates, and Ulysse was apparently quite happy with the little children, who were beautiful and active, although kept dirty and ragged as a protection from the evil eye.

Somehow the engrossing occupation of every one, especially of the only two creatures with whom he could converse, made Arthur more desolate than ever. He lay down under an ilex, and his heart ached with a sick longing he had not experienced since he had been with the Nithsdales, for his mother and his home—the tall narrow-gabled house that had sprung up close to the grim old peel tower, the smell of the sea, the tinkling of the burn. He fell asleep in the heat of the day, and it was to him as if he were once more sitting by the old shepherd on the braeside, hearing him tell the old tales of Johnnie Armstrong or Willie o' the wudspurs.

Actually a Scottish voice was in his ears, as he looked up and saw the turbaned head of Yusuf the merchant bending over him, and saying—'Wake up, my bonny laddie; we can hae our crack in peace while these folks are taking their noonday sleep. Awed, and where are ye frae, and how do you ca' yersel'?'

'I am from Berwickshire,' responded the youth, and as the man started—'My name is Arthur Maxwell Hope of Burnside.'

'Eh! No a son of auld Sir Davie?'

'His youngest son.'

The man clasped his hands, and uttered a strange sound as if in the extremity of amazement, and there was a curious unconscious change of tone, as he said —'Sir Davie's son! Ye'll never have heard tell of Partan Jeannie?' he added.

'A very old fishwife,' said Arthur, 'who used to come her rounds to our door? Was she of kin to you?'

'My mither, sir. Mony's the time I hae peepit out on the cuddie's back between the creels at the door of the braw house of Burnside, and mony's the bannock and cookie the gude lady gied me. My minnie'll no be living thae noo,' he added, not very tenderly.

'I should fear not,' said Arthur. 'I had not seen or heard of her for some time before I left home, and that is now three years since. She looked very old then, and I remember my mother saying she was not fit to come her rounds.'

'She wasna that auld,' returned the merchant gravely; 'but she had led sic a life as falls to the lot of nae wife in this country.'

Arthur had almost said, 'Whose fault was that?' but he durst not offend a possible protector, and softened his words into, 'It is strange to find you here, and a Mohammedan too.'

'Hoots, Maister Arthur, let that flea stick by the wa'. We maun do at Rome as Rome does, as ye'll soon find'—and disregarding Arthur's exclamation —'and the bit bairn, I thocht ye said he was no Scot, when I was daundering awa' at the French yestreen.'

'No, he is half-Irish, half-French, eldest son of Count Burke, a good Jacobite, who got into trouble with the Prince of Orange, and is high in the French service.'

'And what gars your father's son to be *secretaire*, as ye ca'd it, to Frenchman or Irishman either?'

'Well, it was my own fault. I was foolish enough to run away from school to join the rising for our own King's—'

'Eh, sirs! And has there been a rising on the Border side against the English pock puddings? Oh, gin I had kenned it!'

Yusuf's knowledge of English politics had been dim at the best, and he had apparently left Scotland before even Queen Anne was on the throne. When he understood Arthur's story, he communicated his own. He had been engaged in a serious brawl with some English fishers, and in fear of the consequences had fled from Eyemouth, and after casting about as a common sailor in various merchant ships, had been captured by a Moorish vessel, and had found it expedient to purchase his freedom by conversion to Islam, after which his Scottish shrewdness and thrift had resulted in his becoming a prosperous itinerant merchant, with his headquarters at Bona. He expressed himself willing and anxious to do all he could for his young countryman; but it would be almost impossible to do so unless Arthur would accept the religion of his captors; and he explained that the two boys were the absolute property of the tribe, who had discovered and rescued them when going to the seashore to gather kelp for the glass work practised by the Moors in their little furnaces.

'Forsake my religion? Never!' cried Arthur indignantly.

'Saftly, saftly,' said Yusuf; 'nae doot ye trow as I did that they are a' mere pagans and savage heathens, worshipping Baal and Ashtaroth, but I fand myself quite mista'en. They hae no idols, and girn at the blinded Papists as muckle as auld Deacon Shortcoats himsel'.'

'I know that,' threw in Arthur.

'Ay, and they are a hantle mair pious and devout than ever a body I hae seen in Eyemouth, or a' the country side to boot; forbye, my minnie's auld auntie, that sat graning by the ingle, and ay banned us when we came ben. The meneester himsel' dinna gae about blessing and praying over ilka sma' matter like the meenest of us here, and for a' the din they make at hame about the honorable Sabbath, wha thinks of praying five times the day? While as for being the waur for liquor, these folks kenna the very taste of it. Put yon sheyk down on the wharf at Eyemouth, and what wad he say to the Christian folk there?'

A shock of conviction passed over Arthur, though he tried to lose it in indignant defence; but Yusuf did not venture to stay any longer with him, and bidding him think over what had been said, since slavery or Islam were the only alternatives, returned to the tents of merchandise.

First thoughts with the youth had of course been of horror at the bare idea of apostacy, and yet as he watched his Moorish hosts, he could not but own to himself that he never had dreamt that to be among them would be so like dwelling under the oak of Mamre, in the tents of Abraham. From what he remembered of Partan Jeannie's reputation as a being only tolerated and assisted by his mother, on account of her extreme misery and destitution, he could believe that the ne'er-do-weel son, who must have forsaken her before he himself was born, might have really been raised in morality by association with the grave, faithful, and temperate followers of Mohammed, rather than the scum of the port of Eyemouth.

For himself and the boy, what did slavery mean? He hoped to understand better from Yusuf, and at any rate to persuade the man to become the medium of communication with the outside world, beyond that 'dissociable ocean,' over which his wistful gaze wandered. Then the ransom of the little Chevalier de Bourke would be certain, and, if there were any gratitude in the world, his own. But how long would this take, and what might befall them in the meantime?

Ulysse all this time seemed perfectly happy with the small Moors, who all romped together without distinction of rank, of master, slave or colour, for Yusuf's little negro was freely received among them. At night, however, Ulysse's old home self seemed to revive; he crept back to Arthur, tired and weary, fretting for mother, sister, and home; and even after he had fallen asleep, waking again to cry for Julienne. Poor Arthur, he was a rough nurse, but pity kept him patient, and he was even glad to see that the child had not forgotten his home.

Meantime, ever since the sunset prayer, there had been smoking of pipes and drinking of coffee, and earnest discussion between the sheyk and the merchant, and by and by Yusuf came and sat himself down by Arthur, smiling a little at the young man's difficulty in disposing of those long legs upon the ground.

'Ye'll have to learn this and other things, sir,' said he, as he crossed his own under him, Eastern fashion; but his demeanour was on the whole that of the fisher to the laird's son, and he evidently thought that he had a grand proposal to make, for which Master Arthur ought to be infinitely obliged.

He explained to Arthur that Sheyk Abou Ben Zegri had never had more than two sons, and that both had been killed the year before in trying to recover their cattle from the Cabeleyzes, 'a sort of Hieland caterans.'

The girl whom Arthur had noticed was the widow of the elder of the two, and the child was only a daughter. The sheyk had been much impressed by Arthur's exploit in swimming or floating round the headland and saving the child, and regarded his height as something gigantic. Moreover, Yusuf had asserted that he was son to a great Bey in his own country, and in consequence Abou Ben Zegri was willing to adopt him as his son, provided he would embrace the true faith, and marry Ayesha, the widow.

'And,' said Yusuf, 'these women are no that ill for wives, as I ken owre weel'—and he sighed. 'I had as gude and douce a wee wifie at Bona as heart culd wish, and twa bonny bairnies; but when I cam' back frae my rounds, the plague had been there before me. They were a' gone, even Ali, that had just began to ca' me Ab, Ab, and I hae never had heart to gang back to the town house. She was a gude wife—nae flying, nae rampauging. She wad hae died wi' shame to be likened to thae randy wives at hame. Ye might do waur than tak' such a fair offer, Maister Arthur.'

'You mean it all kindly,' said Arthur, touched; 'but for nothing—no, for nothing, can a Christian deny his Lord, or yield up his hopes for hereafter.'

'As for that,' returned Yusuf, 'the meneester and Beacon Shortcoats, and my auld auntie, and the lave of them, aye ca'ed me a vessel of destruction. That was the best name they had for puir Tam. So what odds culd it mak, if I took up with the Prophet, and I was ower lang leggit to row in a galley? Forbye, here they say that a man who prays and gies awmous, and keeps frae wine, is sicker to win to Paradise and a' the houris. I had rather it war my puir Zorah than any strange houri of them a'; but any way, I hae been a better man sin' I took up wi' them than ever I was as a cursing, swearing, drunken, fechting sailor lad wha feared neither God nor devil.'

'That was scarce the fault of the Christian faith,' said Arthur.

'Aweel, the first answer in the Shorter Carritch was a' they ever garred me learn, and that is what we here say of Allah. I see no muckle to choose, and I *ken* ane thing,—it is a hell on earth at ance gin ye gang not alang wi' them. And that's sicker, as ye'll find to your cost, sir, gin ye be na the better guided.'

'With hope, infinite hope beyond,' said Arthur, trying to fortify himself. 'No, I cannot, cannot deny my Lord—my Lord that bought me!'

'We own Issa Ben Mariam for a Prophet,' said Yusuf.

'But He is my only Master, my Redeemer, and God. No, come what may, I can never renounce Him,' said Arthur with vehemence.

'Wed, awed,' said Yusuf, 'maybe ye'll see in time what's for your gude. I'll tell the sheyk it would misbecome your father's son to do sic a deed owre lichtly, and strive to gar him wait while I am in these parts to get your word, and nae doot it will be wiselike at the last.'

CHAPTER VII—MASTER AND SLAVE

'I only heard the reckless waters roar,
Those waves that would not hear me from the shore;
I only marked the glorious sun and sky
Too bright, too blue for my captivity,
And felt that all which Freedom's bosom cheers,
Must break my chain before it dried my tears.'

BYRON (*The Corsair*).

At the rate at which the traffic in Yusuf's tent proceeded, Arthur Hope was likely to have some little time for deliberation on the question presented to him whether to be a free Moslem sheyk or a Christian slave.

Not only had almost every household in El Arnieh to chaffer with the merchant for his wares and to dispose of home-made commodities, but from other adowaras and from hill-farms Moors and Cabyles came in with their produce of wax, wool or silk, to barter—if not with Yusuf, with the inhabitants of El Arnieh, who could weave and embroider, forge cutlery, and make glass from the raw material these supplied. Other Cabyles, divers from the coast, came up, with coral and sponges, the latter of which was the article in which Yusuf preferred to deal, though nothing came amiss to him that he could carry, or that could carry itself—such as a young foal; even the little black boy had been taken on speculation—and so indeed had the big Abyssinian, who, though dumb, was the most useful, ready, and alert of his five slaves. Every bargain seemed to occupy at least an hour, and perhaps Yusuf lingered the longer in order to give Arthur more time for consideration; or it might be that his native tongue, once heard, exercised an irresistible fascination over him. He never failed to have what he called a 'crack' with his young countryman at the hour of the siesta, or at night, perhaps persuading the sheyk that it was controversial, though it was more apt to be on circumstances of the day's trade or the news of the Border-side. Controversy indeed there could be little with one so ignorant as kirk treatment in that century was apt to leave the outcasts of society, nor had conversion to Islam given him much instruction in its tenets; so that the conversation generally was on earthly topics, though it always ended in assurances that Master Arthur would suffer for it if he did not perceive what was for his good. To which Arthur replied to the effect that he must suffer rather than deny his faith; and Yusuf, declaring that a wilful man maun have his way, and that he would rue it too late, went off affronted, but always returned to the charge at the next opportunity.

Meantime Arthur was free to wander about unmolested and pick up the language, in which, however, Ulysse made far more rapid progress, and could be heard chattering away as fast, if not as correctly, as if it were French or English. The delicious climate and the open-air life were filling the little fellow with a strength and vigour unknown to him in a Parisian salon, and he was in the highest spirits among his brown playfellows, ceasing to pine for his mother and sister; and though he still came to Arthur for the night, or in any trouble, it was more and more difficult to get him to submit to be washed and dressed in his tight European clothes, or to say his prayers. He was always sleepy at night and volatile in the morning, and could not be got to listen to the little instructions with which Arthur tried to arm him against Mohammedanism into which the poor little fellow was likely to drift as ignorantly and unconsciously as Yusuf himself.

And what was the alternative? Arthur himself never wavered, nor indeed actually felt that he had a choice; but the prospect before him was gloomy, and Yusuf did not soften it. The sheyk would sell him, and he would either be made to work in some mountain-farm, or put on board a galley; and Yusuf had sufficient experience of the horrors of the latter to assure him emphatically that the gude leddy of Burnside would break her heart to think of her bonny laddie there.

'It would more surely break her heart to think of her son giving up his faith,' returned Arthur.

As to the child, the opinion of the tribe seemed to be that he was just fit to be sent to the Sultan to be bred as a Janissary. 'He will come that gate to be as great a man as in his ain countree,' said Yusuf; 'wi' horse to ride, and sword to bear, and braws to wear, like King Solomon in all his glory.'

'While his father and mother would far rather he were lying dead with her under the waves in that cruel bay,' returned Arthur.

'Hout, mon, ye dinna ken what's for his gude, nor for your ain neither,' retorted Yusuf.

'Good here is not good hereafter.'

'The life of a dog and waur here,' muttered Yusuf; 'ye'll mind me when it is too late.'

'Nay, Yusuf, if you will only take word of our condition to Algiers, we shall —at least the boy—be assuredly redeemed, and you would win a high reward.'

'I am no free to gang to Algiers,' said Yusuf. 'I fell out with a loon there, one of those Janissaries that gang hectoring aboot as though the world were not gude enough for them, and if I hadna made the best of my way out of the toon, my pow wad be a worricow on the wa's of the tower.'

'There are French at Bona, you say. Remember, I ask you to put yourself in no danger, only to bear the tidings to any European,' entreated Arthur.

'And how are they to find ye?' demanded Yusuf. 'Abou Ben Zegri will never keep you here after having evened his gude-daughter to ye. He'll sell you to some corsair captain, and then the best that could betide ye wad be that a shot frae the Knights of Malta should make quick work wi' ye. Or look at the dumbie there, Fareek. A Christian, he ca's himsel', too, though 'tis of a by ordinar' fashion, such as Deacon Shortcoats would scarce own. I coft him dog cheap at Tunis, when his master, the Vizier, had had his tongue cut out— for but knowing o' some deed that suld ne'er have been done—and his puir feet bastinadoed to a jelly. Gin a' the siller in the Dey's treasury ransomed ye, what gude would it do ye after that?'

'I cannot help that—I cannot forsake my God. I must trust Him not to forsake me.'

And, as usual, Yusuf went off angrily muttering, 'He that will to Cupar maun to Cupar.'

Perhaps Arthur's resistance had begun more for the sake of honour, and instinctive clinging to hereditary faith, without the sense of heroism or enthusiasm for martyrdom which sustained Estelle, and rather with the feeling that inconstancy to his faith and his Lord would be base and disloyal. But, as the long days rolled on, if the future of toil and dreary misery developed itself before him, the sense of personal love and aid towards the Lord and Master whom he served grew upon him. Neither the gazelle-eyed Ayesha nor the prosperous village life presented any great temptation. He would have given them all for one bleak day of mist on a Border moss; it was the appalling contrast with the hold of a Moorish galley that at times startled him, together with the only too great probability that he should be utterly incapable of saving poor little Ulysse from unconscious apostacy.

Once Yusuf observed, that if he would only make outward submission to Moslem law, he might retain his own belief and trust in the Lord he seemed so much to love, and of whom he said more good than any Moslem did of the Prophet.

'If I deny Him, He will deny me,' said Arthur.

'And will na He forgive ane as is hard pressed?' asked Yusuf.

'It is a very different thing to go against the light, as I should be doing,' said Arthur, 'and what it might be for that poor bairn, whom Cod preserve.'

'And wow! sir. 'Tis far different wi' you that had the best of gude learning frae the gude leddy,' muttered Yusuf. 'My minnie aye needit me to sort the fish and gang her errands, and wad scarce hae sent me to scule, gin I wad hae gane where they girned at me for Partan Jeannie's wean, and gied me mair o' the tawse than of the hornbook. Gin the Lord, as ye ca' Him, had ever seemed to me what ye say He is to you, Maister Arthur, I micht hae thocht twice o'er the matter. But there's nae ganging back the noo. A Christian's life they harm na, though they mak' it a mere weariness to him; but for him that quits the Prophet, tearing the flesh wi' iron cleeks is the best they hae for him.'

This time Yusuf retreated, not as usual in anger, but as if the bare idea he had broached was too terrible to be dwelt upon. He had by the end of a fortnight completed all his business at El Arnieh, and Arthur, having by this time picked up enough of the language to make himself comprehensible, and to know fully what was set before him, was called upon to make his decision, so that either he might be admitted by regular ritual into the Moslem faith, and adopted by the sheyk, or else be advertised by Yusuf at the next town as a strong young slave.

Sitting in the gate among the village magnates, like an elder of old, Sheyk Abou Ben Zegri, with considerable grace and dignity, set the choice before the Son of the Sea in most affectionate terms, asking of him to become the child of his old age, and to heal the breach left by the swords of the robbers of the mountains.

The old man's fine dark eyes filled with tears, and there was a pathos in his noble manner that made Arthur greatly grieved to disappoint him, and sorry not to have sufficient knowledge of the language to qualify more graciously the resolute reply he had so often rehearsed to himself, expressing his hearty thanks, but declaring that nothing could induce him to forsake the religion of his fathers.

'Wilt thou remain a dog of an unbeliever, and receive the treatment of dogs?'

'I must,' said Arthur.

'The youth is a goodly youth,' said the sheyk; 'it is ill that his heart is blind. Once again, young man, Issa Ben Mariam and slavery, or Mohammed and freedom?'

'I cannot deny my Lord Christ.'

There was a pause. Arthur stood upright, with lips compressed, hands clasped together, while the sheyk and his companions seemed struck by his courage and high spirit. Then one of them—a small, ugly fellow, who had some pretensions to be considered the sheyk's next heir—cried, 'Out on the infidel dog!' and set the example of throwing a handful of dust at him. The crowd who watched around were not slow to follow the example, and Arthur thought he was actually being stoned; but the missiles were for the most part not harmful, only disgusting, blinding, and confusing. There was a tremendous hubbub of vituperation, and he was at last actually stunned by a blow, waking to find himself alone, and with hands and feet bound, in a dirty little shed appropriated to camels. Should he ever be allowed to see poor little Ulysse again, or to speak to Yusuf, in whom lay their only faint hope of redemption? He was helpless, and the boy was at the mercy of the Moors. Was he utterly forsaken?

It was growing late in the day, and he had had no food for many hours. Was he to be neglected and starved? At last he heard steps approaching, and the door was opened by the man who had led the assault on him, who addressed him as 'Son of an old ass—dog of a slave,' bade him stand up and show his height, at the same time cutting the cords that bound him. It was an additional pang that it was to Yusuf that he was thus to exhibit himself, no doubt in order that the merchant should carry a description of him to some likely purchaser. He could not comprehend the words that passed, but it was very bitter to be handled like a horse at a fair—doubly so that he, a Hope of Burnside, should thus be treated by Partan Jeannie's son.

There ensued outside the shrieking and roaring which always accompanied a bargain, and which lasted two full hours. Finally Yusuf looked into the hut, and roughly said in Arabic, 'Come over to me, dog; thou art mine. Kiss the shoe of thy master'—adding in his native tongue, 'For ance, sir. It maun be done before these loons.'

Certainly the ceremony would have been felt as less humiliating towards almost anybody else, but Arthur endured it; and then was led away to the tents beyond the gate.

'There, sir,' said Yusuf, 'it ill sorts your father's son to be in sic a case, but it canna be helpit. I culd na leave behind the bonny Scots tongue, let alane the gude Leddy Hope's son.'

'You have been very good to me, Yusuf,' said Arthur, his pride much softened by the merchant's evident sense of the situation. 'I know you mean me well, but the boy—'

'Hoots! the bairn is happy eno'. He will come to higher preferment than even you or I. Why, mon, an Aga of the Janissaries is as good as the Deuk himsel'.'

'Yusuf, I am very grateful—I believe you must have paid heavily to spare me from ill usage.'

'Ye may say that, sir. Forty piastres of Tunis, and eight mules, and twa pair of silver-mounted pistols. The extortionate rogue wad hae had the little dagger, but I stood out against that.'

'I see, I am deeply beholden,' said Arthur; 'but it would be tenfold better if you would take him instead of me!'

'What for suld I do that? He is nae countryman of mine—one side French and the other Irish. He is naught to me.'

'He is heir to a noble house,' waged Arthur. 'They will reward you amply for saving him.'

'Mair like to girn at me for a Moor. Na, na! Hae na I dune enough for ye, Maister Arthur—giving half my beasties, and more than half my silver? Canna ye be content without that whining bairn?'

'I should be a forsworn man to be content to leave the child, whose dead mother prayed me to protect him, and those who will turn him from her faith. See, now, I am a man, and can guard myself, by the grace of God; but to leave the poor child here would be letting these men work their will on him ere any ransom could come. His mother would deem it giving him up to perdition. Let me remain here, and take the helpless child. You know how to bargain. His price might be my ransom.'

'Ay, when the jackals and hyenas have picked your banes, or you have died under the lash, chained to the oar, as I hae seen, Maister Arthur.'

'Better so than betray the dead woman's trust. How no—'

For there was a pattering of feet, a cry of 'Arthur, Arthur!' and sobbing, screaming, and crying, Ulysse threw himself on his friend's breast. He was pursued by one or two of the hangers-on of the sheyk's household, and the first comer seized him by the arm; but he clung to Arthur, screamed and kicked, and the old nurse who had come hobbling after coaxed in vain. He cried out in a mixture of Arabic and French that he *would* sleep with Arthur—Arthur must put him to bed; no one should take him away.

'Let him stay,' responded Yusuf; 'his time will come soon enough.'

Indulgence to children was the rule, and there was an easy good-nature about the race, which made them ready to defer the storm, and acquiesce in the poor little fellow remaining for another evening with that last remnant of his home to whom he always reverted at nightfall.

He held trembling by Arthur till all were gone, then looked about in terror, and required to be assured that no one was coming to take him away.

'They shall not,' he cried. 'Arthur, you will not leave me alone? They are all gone—Mamma, and Estelle, and *la bonne*, and Laurent, and my uncle, and all, and you will not go.'

'Not now, not to-night, my dear little mannie,' said Arthur, tears in his eyes for the first time throughout these misfortunes.

'Not now! No, never!' said the boy hugging him almost to choking. 'That naughty Ben Kader said they had sold you for a slave, and you were going away; but I knew I should find you—you are not a slave!—you are not black —'

'Ah! Ulysse, it is too true; I am—'

'No! no! no!' the child stamped, and hung on him in a passion of tears. 'You shall not be a slave. My papa shall come with his soldiers and set you free.'

Altogether the boy's vehemence, agitation, and terror were such that Arthur found it impossible to do anything but soothe and hush him, as best might be, till his sobs subsided gradually, still heaving his little chest even after he fell asleep in the arms of his unaccustomed nurse, who found himself thus baffled in using this last and only opportunity of trying to strengthen the child's faith, and was also hindered from pursuing Yusuf, who had left the tent. And if it were separation that caused all this distress, what likelihood that Yusuf would encumber himself with a child who had shown such powers of wailing and screaming?

He durst not stir nor speak for fear of wakening the boy, even when Yusuf returned and stretched himself on his mat, drawing a thick woollen cloth over him, for the nights were chill. Long did Arthur lie awake under the strange sense of slavery and helplessness, and utter uncertainty as to his fate, expecting, in fact, that Yusuf meant to keep him as a sort of tame animal to talk Scotch; but hoping to work on him in time to favour an escape, and at any rate to despatch a letter to Algiers, as a forlorn hope for the ultimate redemption of the poor little unconscious child who lay warm and heavy across his breast. Certainly, Arthur had never so prayed for aid, light, and deliverance as now!

CHAPTER VIII—THE SEARCH

'The lights begin to twinkle from the rocks,
The long day wanes, the slow moon climbs. The deep
Moans round with many voices. Come, my friends.'

TENNYSON.

Arthur fell asleep at last, and did not waken till after sunrise, nor did Ulysse, who must have been exhausted with crying and struggling. When they did awaken, Arthur thinking with heavy heart that the moment of parting was come, he saw indeed the other three slaves busied in making bales of the merchandise; but the master, as well as the Abyssinian, Fareek, and the little negro were all missing. Bekir, who was a kind of foreman, and looked on the new white slave with some jealousy, roughly pointed to some coarse food, and in reply to the question whether the merchant was taking leave of the sheyk, intimated that it was no business of theirs, and assumed authority to make his new fellow-slave assist in the hardest of the packing.

Arthur had no heart to resist, much as it galled him to be ordered about by this rude fellow. It was only a taste, as he well knew, of what he had embraced, and he was touched by poor little Ulysse's persistency in keeping as close as possible, though his playfellows came down and tried first to lure, then to drag him away, and finally remained to watch the process of packing up. Though Bekir was too disdainful to reply to his fellow-slave's questions, Arthur picked up from answers to the Moors who came down that Yusuf had recollected that he had not finished his transactions with a little village of Cabyle coral and sponge-fishers on the coast, and had gone down thither, taking the little negro, to whom the headman seemed to have taken a fancy, so as to become a possible purchaser, and with the Abyssinian to attend to the mules.

A little before sundown Yusuf returned. Fareek lifted down a pannier covered by a crimson and yellow kerchief, and Yusuf declared, with much apparent annoyance, that the child was sick, and that this had frustrated the sale. He was asleep, must be carried into the tent, and not disturbed: for though the Cabyles had not purchased him, there was no affording to loose anything of so much value. Moreover, observing Ulysse still hovering round the Scot, he said, 'You may bide here the night, laddie, I ha tell't the sheyk;' and he repeated the same to the slaves in Arabic, dismissing them to hold a parting feast on a lamb stuffed with pistachio nuts, together with their village friends.

Then drawing near to Arthur, he said, 'Can ye gar yon wean keep a quiet sough, if we make him pass for the little black?'

Arthur started with joy, and stammered some words of intense relief and gratitude.

'The deed's no dune yet,' said Yusuf, 'and it is ower like to end in our leaving a' our banes on the sands! But a wilfu' man maun have his way,' he repeated; 'so, sir, if it be your wull, ye'd better speak to the bairn, for we must make a blackamoor of him while there is licht to do it, or Bekir, whom I dinna lippen to, comes back frae the feast.'

Ulysse, being used to Irish-English, had little understanding of Yusuf's broad Scotch; but he was looking anxiously from one to the other of the speakers, and when Arthur explained to him that the disguise, together with perfect silence, was the only hope of not being left behind among the Moors, and the best chance of getting back to his home and dear ones again, he perfectly understood. As to the blackening, for which Yusuf had prepared a mixture to be laid on with a feather, it was perfectly enchanting to *faire la comedie*. He laughed so much that he had to be peremptorily hushed, and they were sensible of the danger that in case of a search he might betray himself to his Moorish friends; and Arthur tried to make him comprehend the extreme danger, making him cry so that his cheeks had to be touched up. His eyes and hair were dark, and the latter was cut to its shortest by Yusuf, who further managed to fasten some tufts of wool dipped in the black unguent to the kerchief that bound his head. The childish features had something of the Irish cast, which lent itself to the transformation, and in the scanty garments of the little negro Arthur owned that he should never have known the small French gentleman. Arthur was full of joy—Yusuf gruff, brief, anxious, like one acting under some compulsion most unwillingly, and even despondently, but apparently constrained by a certain instinctive feudal feeling, which made him follow the desires of the young Border laird's son.

All had been packed beforehand, and there was nothing to be done but to strike the tents, saddle the mules, and start. Ulysse, still very sleepy, was lifted into the pannier, almost at the first streak of dawn, while the slaves were grumbling at being so early called up; and to a Moor who wakened up and offered to take charge of the little Bey, Yusuf replied that the child had been left in the sheyk's house.

So they were safely out at the outer gate, and proceeding along a beautiful path leading above the cliffs. The mules kept in one long string, Bekir with the foremost, which was thus at some distance from the hindmost, which carried Ulysse and was attended by Arthur, while the master rode his own animals and gave directions. The fiction of illness was kept up, and when the bright eyes looked up in too lively a manner, Yusuf produced some of the sweets, which were always part of his stock in trade, as a bribe to quietness.

At sunrise, the halt for prayer was a trial to Arthur's intense anxiety, and far more so was the noontide one for sleep. He even ventured a remonstrance, but was answered, 'Mair haste, worse speed. Our lives are no worth a boddle till the search is over.'

They were on the shady side of a great rock overhung by a beautiful creeping plant, and with a spring near at hand, and Yusuf, in leisurely fashion, squatted down, caused Arthur to lift out the child, who was fast asleep again, and the mules to be allowed to feed, and distributed some dried goat's flesh and dates; but Ulysse, somewhat to Arthur's alarm, did not wake sufficiently to partake.

Looking up in alarm, he met a sign from Yusuf and presently a whisper, 'No hurt done—'tis safer thus—'

And by this time there were alarming sounds on the air. The sheyk and two of the chief men of El Arnieh were on horseback and armed with matchlocks; and the whole *'posse* of the village were following on foot, with yells and vituperations of the entire ancestry of the merchant, and far more complicated and furious threats than Arthur could follow; but he saw Yusuf go forward to meet them with the utmost cool courtesy.

They seemed somewhat discomposed: Yusuf appeared to condole with them on the loss, and, waving his hands, put all his baggage at their service for a search, letting them run spears through the bales, and overturn the baskets of sponges, and search behind every rock. When they approached the sleeping boy, Arthur, with throbbing heart, dimly comprehended that Yusuf was repeating the story of the disappointment of a purchase caused by his illness, and lifting for a moment the covering laid over him to show the bare black legs and arms. There might also have been some hint of infection which, in spite of all Moslem belief in fate, deterred Abou Ben Zegri from an over-close inspection. Yusuf further invented a story of having put the little Frank in charge of a Moorish woman in the adowara; but added he was so much attached to the Son of the Sea, that most likely he had wandered out in search of him, and the only wise course would be to seek him before he was devoured by any of the wild beasts near home.

Nevertheless, there was a courteous and leisurely smoking of pipes and drinking of coffee before the sheyk and his followers turned homewards. To Arthur's alarm and surprise, however, Yusuf did not resume the journey, but told Bekir that there would hardly be a better halting-place within their powers, as the sun was already some way on his downward course; and besides, it would take some time to repack the goods which had been cast about in every direction during the search. The days were at their shortest, though that was not very short, closing in at about five o'clock, so that there was not much time to spare. Arthur began to feel some alarm at the continued drowsiness of the little boy, who only once muttered something, turned round, and slept again.

'What have you done to him?' asked Arthur anxiously.

'The poppy,' responded Yusuf. 'Never fash yoursel'. The bairn willna be a hair the waur, and 'tis better so than that he shuld rax a' our craigs.'

Yusuf's peril was so much the greater, that it was impossible to object to any of his precautions, especially as he might take offence and throw the whole matter over; but it was impossible not to chafe secretly at the delay, which seemed incomprehensible. Indeed, the merchant was avoiding private communication with Arthur, only assuming the master, and ordering about in a peremptory fashion which it was very hard to digest.

After the sunset orisons had been performed, Yusuf regaled his slaves with a donation of coffee and tobacco, but with a warning to Arthur not to partake, and to keep to windward of them. So too did the Abyssinian, and the cause of the warning was soon evident, as Bekir and his companion nodded, and then sank into a slumber as sound as that of the little Frenchman. Indeed, Arthur himself was weary enough to fall asleep soon after sundown, in spite of his anxiety, and the stars were shining like great lamps when Yusuf awoke him. One mule stood equipped beside him, and held by the Abyssinian. Yusuf pointed to the child, and said, 'Lift him upon it.'

Arthur obeyed, finding a pannier empty on one side to receive the child, who only muttered and writhed instead of awaking. The other side seemed laden. Yusuf led the animal, retracing their way, while fire-flies flitted around with their green lights, and the distant laughter of hyenas gave Arthur a thrill of loathing horror. Huge bats fluttered round, and once or twice grim shapes crossed their path.

'Uncanny beasties,' quoth Yusuf; 'but they will soon be behind us.'

He turned into a rapidly-sloping path. Arthur felt a fresh salt breeze in his face, and his heart leapt up with hope.

In about an hour and a half they had reached a cove, shut in by dark rocks which in the night looked immeasurable, but on the white beach a few little huts were dimly discernible, one with a light in it. The sluggish dash of waves could be heard on the shore; there was a sense of infinite space and breadth before them; and Jupiter sitting in the north-west was like an enormous lamp, casting a pathway of light shimmering on the waters to lead the exiles home.

Three or four boats were drawn up on the beach; a man rose up from within one, and words in a low voice were exchanged between him and Yusuf; while Fareek, grinning so that his white teeth could be seen in the starlight, unloaded the mule, placing its packs, a long Turkish blunderbuss, and two skins of water, in the boat, and arranging a mat on which Arthur could lay the sleeping child.

Well might the youth's heart bound with gratitude, as, unmindful of all the further risks and uncertainties to be encountered, he almost saw his way back to Burnside!

CHAPTER IX—ESCAPE

'Beside the helm he sat, steering expert,
Nor sleep fell ever on his eyes that watch'd
Intent the Pleiads, tardy in decline,
Bootes and the Bear, call'd else the Wain,
Which in his polar prison circling, looks
Direct towards Orion, and alone
Of these sinks never to the briny deep.'

Odyssey (COWPER).

The boat was pushed off, the Abyssinian leapt into it; Arthur paused to pour
out his thankfulness to Yusuf, but was met with the reply, 'Hout awa'! Time
enough for that—in wi' ye.' And fancying there was some alarm, he sprang in,
and to his amazement found Yusuf instantly at his side, taking the rudder, and
giving some order to Fareek, who had taken possession of a pair of oars;
while the waters seemed to flash and glitter a welcome at every dip.

'You are coming! you are coming!' exclaimed Arthur, clasping the merchant's
hand, almost beside himself with joy.

'Sma' hope wad there be of a callant like yersel' and the wean there winning
awa' by yer lane,' growled Yusuf.

'You have given up all for us.'

'There wasna muckle to gie,' returned the sponge merchant. 'Sin' the
gudewife and her bit bairnies at Bona were gane, I hadna the heart to gang
thereawa', nor quit the sound o' the bonny Scots tongue. I wad as soon gang
to the bottom as to the toom house. For dinna ye trow yersells ower sicker
e'en the noo.'

'Is there fear of pursuit?'

'No mickle o' that. The folk here are what they ca' Cabyles, a douce set, not
forgathering with Arabs nor wi' Moors. I wad na gang among them till the
search was over to-day; but yesterday I saw yon carle, and coft the boatie frae
him for the wee blackamoor and the mule. The Moors at El Aziz are not
seafaring; and gin the morn they jalouse what we have done, we have the start
of them. Na, I'm not feared for them; but forbye that, this is no the season for
an open boatie wi' a crew of three and a wean. Gin we met an Algerian or
Tunisian cruiser, as we are maist like to do, a bullet or drooning wad be ower

gude in their e'en for us—for me, that is to say. They wad spare the bairn, and may think you too likely a lad to hang on the walls like a split corbie on the woodsman's lodge.'

'Well, Yusuf, my name is Hope, you know,' said Arthur. 'God has brought us so far, and will scarce leave us now. I feel three times the man that I was when I lay down this evening. Do we keep to the north, where we are sure to come to a Christian land in time?'

'Easier said than done. Ye little ken what the currents are in this same sea, or deed ye'll soon ken when we get into them.'

Arthur satisfied himself that they were making for the north by looking at the Pole Star, so much lower than he was used to see it in Scotland that he hardly recognised his old friend; but, as he watched the studded belt of the Hunter and the glittering Pleiades, the Horatian dread of *Nimbosus Orion* occurred to him as a thought to be put away.

Meantime there was a breeze from the land, and the sail was hoisted. Yusuf bade both Arthur and Fareek lie down to sleep, for their exertions would be wanted by and by, since it would not be safe to use the sail by daylight. It was very cold—wild blasts coming down from the mountains; but Arthur crept under the woollen mantle that had been laid over Ulysse, and was weary enough to sleep soundly. Both were awakened by the hauling down of the mast; and the little boy, who had quite slept off the drug, scrambling out from under the covering, was astonished beyond measure at finding himself between the glittering, sparkling expanse of sea and the sky, where the sun had just leapt up in a blaze of gold.

The white summits of Atlas were tipped with rosy light, beautiful to behold, though the voyagers had much rather have been out of sight of them.

'How much have we made, Yusuf?' began Arthur.

'Tam Armstrong, so please you, sir! Yusuf's dead and buried the noo; and if I were farther beyant the grip of them that kenned him, my thrapple would feel all the sounder!'

This day was, he further explained, the most perilous one, since they were by no means beyond the track of vessels plying on the coast; and as a very jagged and broken cluster of rocks lay near, he decided on availing themselves of the shelter they afforded. The boat was steered into a narrow channel between two which stood up like the fangs of a great tooth, and afforded a pleasant shade; but there was such a screaming and calling of gulls, terns, cormorants, and all manner of other birds, as they entered the little strait, and such a cloud of them hovered and whirled overhead, that Tam

99

uttered imprecations on their skirling, and bade his companions lie close and keep quiet till they had settled again, lest the commotion should betray that the rocks were the lair of fugitives.

It was not easy to keep Ulysse quiet, for he was in raptures at the rush of winged creatures, and no less so at the wonderful sea-anemones and starfish in the pools, where long streamers of weed of beautiful colours floated on the limpid water.

Nothing reduced him to stillness but the sight of the dried goat's flesh and dates that Tam Armstrong produced, and for which all had appetites, which had to be checked, since no one could tell how long it would be before any kind of haven could be reached.

Arthur bathed himself and his charge in a pool, after Tam had ascertained that no many-armed squid or cuttlefish lurked within it. And while Ulysse disported himself like a little fish, Arthur did his best to restore him to his natural complexion, and tried to cleanse the little garments, which showed only too plainly the lack of any change, and which were the only Frank or Christian clothes among them, since young Hope himself had been almost stripped when he came ashore, and wore the usual garb of Yusuf's slaves.

Presently Fareek made an imperative sign to hush the child's merry tongue; and peering forth in intense anxiety, the others perceived a lateen sail passing perilously near, but happily keeping aloof from the sharp reef of rocks around their shelter. Arthur had forgotten the child's prayers and his own, but Ulysse connected them with dressing, and the alarm of the passing ship had recalled them to the young man's mind, though he felt shy as he found that Tam Armstrong was not asleep, but was listening and watching with his keen gray eyes under their grizzled brows. Presently, when Ulysse was dropping to sleep again, the ex-merchant began to ask questions with the intelligence of his shrewd Scottish brains.

The stern Calvinism of the North was wont to consign to utter neglect the outcast border of civilisation, where there were no decent parents to pledge themselves; and Partan Jeannie's son had grown up well-nigh in heathen ignorance among fisher lads and merchant sailors, till it had been left for him to learn among the Mohammedans both temperance and devotional habits. His whole faith and understanding would have been satisfied for ever; but there had been strange yearnings within him ever since he had lost his wife and children, and these had not passed away when Arthur Hope came in his path. Like many another renegade, he could not withstand the attraction of his native tongue; and in this case it was doubled by the feudal attachment of the district to the family of Burnside, and a grateful remembrance of the lady who had been one of the very few persons who had ever done a kindly deed by the little outcast. He had broken with all his Moslem ties for Arthur Hope's sake; and these being left behind, he began to make some inquiries about that Christian faith to which he must needs return—if return be the right word in the case of one who knew it so little when he had abjured it.

And Arthur had not been bred to the grim reading of the doctrine of predestination which had condemned poor Tam, even before he had embraced the faith of the Prophet. Boyish, and not over thoughtful, the youth, when brought face to face with apostacy, had been ready to give life or liberty rather than deny his Lord; and deepened by that great decision, he could hold up that Lord and Redeemer in colours that made Tam see that his clinging to his faith was not out of mere honour and constancy, but that Mohammed had been a poor and wretched substitute for Him whom the poor fellow had denied, not knowing what he did.

'Weel!' he said, 'gin the Deacon and the auld aunties had tellt me as mickle about Him, thae Moors might ha' preached their thrapples sair for Tam. Mashallah! Maister Arthur, do ye think, noo, He can forgie a puir carle for turning frae Him an' disowning Him?'

'I am sure of it, Tam. He forgives all who come to Him—and you—you did it in ignorance.'

'And you trow na that I am a vessel of wrath, as they aye said?'

'No, no, no, Tam. How could that be with one who has done what you have for us? There is good in you—noble goodness, Tam; and who could have put it there but God, the Holy Spirit? I believe myself He was leading you all the time, though you did not know it; making you a better man first, and now, through this brave kindness to us, bringing you back to be a real true Christian and know Him.'

Arthur felt as if something put the words into his mouth, but he felt them with all his heart, and the tears were in his eyes.

At sundown Tam grew restless. Force of habit impelled him to turn to Mecca and make his devotions as usual, and after nearly kneeling down on the flat stone, he turned to Arthur and said, 'I canna wed do without the bit prayer, sir.

'No, indeed, Tam. Only let it be in the right Name.'

And Arthur knelt down beside him and said the Lord's Prayer—then, under a spell of bashfulness, muttered special entreaty for protection and safety.

They were to embark again now that darkness would veil their movements, but the wind blew so much from the north that they could not raise the sail. The oars were taken by Tam and Fareek at first, but when they came into difficult currents Arthur changed places with the former.

And thus the hours passed. The Mediterranean may be in our eyes a European lake, but it was quite large enough to be a desert of sea and sky to the little crew of an open boat, even though they were favoured by the weather. Otherwise, indeed, they must have perished in the first storm. They durst not sail except by night, and then only with northerly winds, nor could there be much rest, since they could not lay to, and drift with the currents, lest they should be carried back to the African coast. Only one of the three men could sleep at a time, and that by one of the others taking both oars, and in time this could not but become very exhausting. It was true that all the coasts to the north were of Christian lands; but in their Moorish garments and in perfect ignorance of Italian, strangers might fare no better in Sardinia or Sicily than in Africa, and Spain might be no better; but Tam endeavoured to keep a north-westerly course, thinking from what Arthur had said that in this direction there was more chance of being picked up by a French vessel. Would their strength and provisions hold out? Of this there was serious doubt. Late in the year as it was, the heat and glare were as distressing by day as was the cold by night, and the continued exertion of rowing produced thirst, which made it very difficult to husband the water in the skins. Tam and Fareek were both tough, and inured to heat and privation; but Arthur, scarce yet come to his full height, and far from having attained proportionate robustness and muscular strength, could not help flagging, though, whenever steering was of minor importance, Tam gave him the rudder, moved by his wan looks, for he never complained, even when fragments of dry goat's flesh almost choked his parched mouth. The boy was never allowed to want for anything save water; but it was very hard to hear him fretting for it. Tam took the goatskin into his own keeping, and more than once uttered a rough reproof, and yet Arthur saw him give the child half his own precious ration when it must have involved grievous suffering. The promise about giving the cup of cold water to a little one could not but rise to his lips.

'Cauld! and I wish it were cauld!' was all the response Tam made; but his face showed some gratification.

This was no season for traffic, and they had barely seen a sail or two in the distance, and these only such as the experienced eyes of the ex-sponge merchant held to be dangerous. Deadly lassitude began to seize the young Scot; he began scarcely to heed what was to become of them, and had not energy to try to console Ulysse, who, having in an unwatched moment managed to swallow some sea water, was crying and wailing under the additional misery he had inflicted on himself. The sun beat down with noontide force, when on that fourth day, turning from its scorching, his languid eye espied a sail on the northern horizon.

'See,' he cried; 'that is not the way of the Moors.'

'Bismillah! I beg your pardon, sir,' cried Tam, but said no more, only looked intently.

Gradually, gradually the spectacle rose on their view fuller and fuller, not the ruddy wings of the Algerine or Italian, but the square white castle-like tiers of sails rising one above another, bearing along in a south-easterly direction.

'English or French,' said Tam, with a long breath, for her colours and build were not yet discernible. 'Mashallah! I beg pardon. I mean, God grant she pass us not by!'

The mast was hastily raised, with Tam's turban unrolled, floating at the top of it; and while he and Fareek plied their oars with might and main, he bade Arthur fire off at intervals the blunderbuss, which had hitherto lain idle at the bottom of the boat.

How long the intense suspense lasted they knew not ere Arthur cried, 'They are slackening sail! Thank God. Tam, you have saved us! English!'

'Not so fast!' Tam uttered an Arabic and then a Scottish interjection.

Their signal had been seen by other eyes. An unmistakable Algerine, with the crescent flag, was bearing down on them from the opposite direction.

'Rascals. Do they not dread the British flag?' cried Arthur. 'Surely that will protect us?'

'They are smaller and lighter, and with their galley slaves can defy the wind, and loup off like a flea in a blanket,' returned Tam, grimly. 'Mair by token, they guess what we are, and will hold on to hae my life's bluid if naething mair! Here! Gie us a soup of the water, and the last bite of flesh. 'Twill serve us the noo, find we shall need it nae mair any way.'

Arthur fed him, for he durst not slacken rowing for a moment. Then seeing Fareek, who had borne the brunt of the fatigue, looking spent, the youth, after swallowing a few morsels and a little foul-smelling drink, took the second oar, while double force seemed given to the long arms lately so weary, and both pulled on in silent, grim desperation. Ulysse had given one scream at seeing the last of the water swallowed, but he too, understood the situation, and obeyed Arthur's brief words, 'Kneel down and pray for us, my boy.'

The Abyssinian was evidently doing the same, after having loaded the blunderbuss; but it was no longer necessary to use this as a signal, since the frigate had lowered her boat, which was rapidly coming towards them.

But, alas! still more swiftly, as it seemed to those terrified eyes, came the Moorish boat—longer, narrower, more favoured by currents and winds, flying like a falcon towards its prey. It was a fearful race. Arthur's head began to swim, his breath to labour, his arms to move stiffly as a thresher's flail; but, just as power was failing him, an English cheer came over the waters, and restored strength for a few more resolute strokes.

Then came some puffs of smoke from the pirate's boat, a report, a jerk to their own, a fresh dash forward, even as Fareek fired, giving a moment's check to the enemy. There was a louder cheer, several shots from the English boat, a cloud from the ship's side. Then Arthur was sensible of a relaxation of effort, and that the chase was over, then that the British boat was alongside, friendly voices ringing in his ears, 'How now, mates? Runaways, eh? Where d'ye hail from?'

'Scottish! British!' panted out Arthur, unable to utter more, faint, giddy, and astounded by the cheers around him, and the hands stretched out in welcome. He scarcely saw or understood.

'Queer customers here! What! a child! Who are you, my little man? And what's this? A Moor! He's hit—pretty hard too.'

This brought back Arthur's reeling senses in one flash of horror, at the sight of Tam, bleeding fast in the bottom of the boat.

'O Tam! Tam! He saved me! He is Scottish too,' cried Arthur. 'Sir, is he alive?'

'I think so,' said the officer, who had bent over Tam. 'We'll have him aboard in a minute, and see what the doctor can do with him. You seem to have had a narrow escape.'

Arthur was too busy endeavouring to staunch the blood which flowed fast from poor Tam's side to make much reply, but Ulysse, perched on the officer's knee, was answering for him in mixed English and French. 'Moi, je suis le Chevalier de Bourke! My papa is ambassador to Sweden. This gentleman is his secretary. We were shipwrecked—and M. Arture and I swam away together. The Moors were good to us, and wanted to make us Moors; but M. Arture said it would be wicked. And Yusuf bought him for a slave; but that was only from *faire la comédie*. He is *bon Chrétien* after all, and so is poor Fareek, only he is dumb. Yusuf—that is, Tam—made me all black, and changed me for his little negro boy; and we got into the boat, and it was very hot, and oh! I am so thirsty. And now M. Arture will take me to Monsieur mon Père, and get me some nice clothes again,' concluded the young gentleman, who, in this moment of return to civilised society, had become perfectly aware of his own rank and importance.

Arthur only looked up to verify the child's statements, which had much struck the lieutenant. Their boat had by this time been towed alongside of the frigate, and poor Tam was hoisted on board, and the surgeon was instantly at hand; but he said at once that the poor fellow was fast dying, and that it would be useless torture to carry him below for examination.

A few words passed with the captain, and then the little Chevalier was led away to tell his own tale, which he was doing with a full sense of his own importance; but presently the captain returned, and beckoned to Arthur, who had been kneeling beside poor Tam, moistening his lips, and bathing his face, as he lay gasping and apparently unconscious, except that he had gripped hold of his broad sash or girdle when it was taken off.

'The child tells me he is Comte de Bourke's son,' said the captain, in a tentative manner, as if doubtful whether he should be understood, and certainly Arthur looked more Moorish than European.

'Yes, sir! He was on his way with his mother to join his father when we were taken by a Moorish corsair.'

'But you are not French?' said the captain, recognising the tones.

'No, sir; Scottish—Arthur Maxwell Hope. I was to have gone as the Count's secretary.'

'You have escaped from the Moors? I could not understand what the boy said. Where are the lady and the rest?'

Arthur as briefly as he could, for he was very anxious to return to poor Tam, explained the wreck and the subsequent adventures, saying that he feared the poor Countess was lost, but that he had seen her daughter and some of her suite on a rock. Captain Beresford was horrified at the idea of a Christian child among the wild Arabs. His station was Minorca, but he had just been at the Bay of Rosas, where poor Comte de Bourke's anxiety and distress about his wife and children were known, and he had received a request amounting to orders to try to obtain intelligence about them, so that he held it to be within his duty to make at once for Djigheli Bay.

For further conversation was cut short by sounds of articulate speech from poor Tam. Arthur turned hastily, and the captain proceeded to give his orders.

'Is Maister Hope here?'

'Here! Yes. O Tam, dear Tam, if I could do anything!' cried Arthur.

'I canna see that well,' said Tam, with a sound of anxiety. 'Where's my sash?'

'This is it, in your own hand,' said Arthur, thinking he was wandering, but the other hand sought one of the ample folds, which was sewn over, and weighty.

'Tak' it; tak' tent of it; ye'll need the siller. Four hunder piastres of Tunis, not countin' zeechins, and other sma' coin.'

'Shall I send them to any one at Eyemouth?'

Tam almost laughed. 'Na, na; keep them and use them yersell, sir. There's nane at hame that wad own puir Tam. The leddy, your mither, an' you hae been mair to me than a' beside that's above ground, and what wad ye do wi'out the siller?'

'O Tam! I owe all and everything to you. And now—'

Tam looked up, as Arthur's utterance was choked, and a great tear fell on his face. 'Wha wad hae said,' murmured he, 'that a son of Burnside wad be greetin' for Partan Jeannie's son?'

'For my best friend. What have you not saved me from! and I can do nothing!'

'Nay, sir. Say but thae words again.'

'Oh for a clergyman! Or if I had a Bible to read you the promises.'

'You shall have one,' said the captain, who had returned to his side. The surgeon muttered that the lad seemed as good as a parson; but Arthur heard him not, and was saying what prayers came to his mind in this stress, when, even as the captain returned, the last struggle came on. Once more Tam looked up, saying, 'Ye'll be good to puir Fareek;' and with a word more, 'Oh, Christ: will He save such as I?' all was over.

'Come away, you can do nothing more,' said the doctor. 'You want looking to yourself.'

For Arthur tottered as he tried to rise, and needed the captain's kind hand as he gained his feet. 'Sir,' he said, as the tears gushed to his eyes, 'he *does* deserve all honour—my only friend and deliverer.'

'I see,' said Captain Beresford, much moved; 'whatever he has been, he died a Christian. He shall have Christian burial. And this fellow?' pointing to poor Fareek, whose grief was taking vent in moans and sobs.

'Christian—Abyssinian, but dumb,' Arthur explained; and having his promise that all respect should be paid to poor Tam's corpse, he let the doctor lead him away, for he had now time to feel how sun-scorched and exhausted he was, with giddy, aching head, and legs cramped and stiff, arms strained and shoulders painful after his three days and nights of the boat. His thirst, too, seemed unquenchable, in spite of drinks almost unconsciously taken, and though hungry he had little will to eat.

The surgeon made him take a warm bath, and then fed him with soup, after which, on a promise of being called in due time, he consented to deposit himself in a hammock, and presently fell asleep.

When he awoke he found that clothes had been provided for him—naval uniforms; but that could not be helped, and the comfort was great. He was refreshed, but still very stiff. However, he dressed and was just ready, when the surgeon came to see whether he were in condition to be summoned, for it was near sundown, and all hands were piped up to attend poor Tam's funeral rites. His generous and faithful deed had eclipsed the memory that he was a renegade, and, indeed, it had been in such ignorance that he had had little to deny.

All the sailors stood as respectfully as if he had been one of themselves while the captain read a portion of the Burial Office. Such honours would never have been his in his native land, where at that time even Episcopalians themselves could not have ventured on any out-door rites; and Arthur was thus doubly struck and impressed, when, as the corpse, sewn in sail-cloth and heavily weighted, was launched into the blue waves, he heard the words committing the body to the deep, till the sea should give up her dead. He longed to be able to translate them to poor Fareek, who was weeping and howling so inconsolably as to attest how good a master he had lost.

Perhaps Tam's newly-found or recovered Christianity might have been put to hard shocks as to the virtues he had learnt among the Moslems. At any rate Arthur often had reason to declare in after life that the poor renegade might have put many a better-trained Christian to shame.

CHAPTER X—ON BOARD THE 'CALYPSO'

'From when this youth?
His country, name, and birth declare!'

SCOTT.

'You had forgotten this legacy, Mr. Hope,' said Captain Beresford, taking Arthur into his cabin, 'and, judging by its weight, it is hardly to be neglected. I put it into my locker for security.'

'Thank you, sir,' said Arthur. 'The question is whether I ought to take it. I wished for your advice.'

'I heard what passed,' said the captain. 'I should call your right as complete as if you had a will made by a half a dozen lawyers. When we get into port, a few crowns to the ship's company to drink your health, and all will be right. Will you count it?'

The folds were undone, and little piles made of the gold, but neither the captain nor Arthur were much the wiser. The purser might have computed it, but Captain Beresford did not propose this, thinking perhaps that it was safer that no report of a treasure should get abroad in the ship.

He made a good many inquiries, which he had deferred till Arthur should be in a fitter condition for answering, first about the capture and wreck, and what the young man had been able to gather about the Cabeleyzes. Then, as the replies showed that he had a gentleman before him, Captain Beresford added that he could not help asking, '*Que diable allait il faire dans cette galère?*'

'Sir,' said Arthur, 'I do not know whether you will think it your duty to make me a prisoner, but I had better tell you the whole truth.'

'Oho!' said the captain; 'but you are too young! You could never have been out with—with—we'll call him the Chevalier.'

'I ran away from school,' replied Arthur, colouring. 'I was a mere boy, and I never was attainted,' explained Arthur, blushing. 'I have been with my Lord Nithsdale, and my mother thought I could safely come home, and that if I came from Sweden my brother could not think I compromised him.'

'Your brother?'

'Lord Burnside. He is at Court, in favour, they say, with King George. He is my half-brother; my mother is a Maxwell.'

'There is a Hope in garrison at Port Mahon—a captain,' said the captain. 'Perhaps he will advise you what to do if you are sick of Jacobite intrigue and mystery, and ready to serve King George.'

Arthur's face lighted up. 'Will it be James Hope of Ryelands, or Dickie Hope of the Lynn, or—?'

Captain Beresford held up his hands.

'Time must show that, my young friend,' he said, smiling. 'And now I think the officers expect you to join their mess in the gunroom.'

There Arthur found the little Chevalier strutting about in an adaptation of the smallest midshipman's uniform, and the centre of an admiring party, who were equally diverted by his consequential airs and by his accounts of his sports among the Moors. Happy fellow, he could adapt himself to any society, and was ready to be the pet and plaything of the ship's company, believing himself, when he thought of anything beyond the present, to be full on the road to his friends again.

Fareek was a much more difficult charge, for Arthur had hardly a word that he could understand. He found the poor fellow coiled up in a corner, just where he had seen his former master's remains disappear, still moaning and weeping bitterly. As Arthur called to him he looked up for a moment, then crawled forward, striking his forehead at intervals against the deck. He was about to kiss the feet of his former fellow-slave, the glittering gold, blue, and white of whose borrowed dress no doubt impressed him. Arthur hastily started back, to the amazement of the spectators, and called out a negative—one of the words sure to be first learnt. He tried to take Fareek's hand and raise him from his abject attitude; but the poor fellow continued kneeling, and not only were no words available to tell him that he was free, but it was extremely doubtful whether freedom was any boon to him. One thing, however, he did evidently understand—he pointed to the St. George's pennant with the red cross, made the sign, looked an interrogation, and on Arthur's reply, 'Christians,' and reiteration of the word 'Salem,' *peace*, he folded his arms and looked reassured.

'Ay, ay, my hearty,' said the big boatswain, 'ye've got under the old flag, and we'll soon make you see the difference. Cut out your poor tongue, have they, the rascals, and made a dummy of you? I wish my cat was about their ears! Come along with you, and you shall find what British grog is made of.'

And a remarkable friendship arose between the two, the boatswain patronising Fareek on every occasion, and roaring at him as if he were deaf as

110

well as dumb, and Fareek appearing quite confident under his protection, and establishing a system of signs, which were fortunately a universal language. The Abyssinian evidently viewed himself as young Hope's servant or slave, probably thinking himself part of his late master's bequest, and there was no common language between them in which to explain the difference or ascertain the poor fellow's wishes. He was a slightly-made, dexterous man, probably about five and twenty years of age, and he caught up very quickly, by imitation, the care he could take of Arthur's clothes, and the habit of waiting on him at meals.

Meantime the *Calypso* held her course to the south-east, till the chart declared the coast to be that of Djigheli Bay, and Arthur recognised the headlands whither the unfortunate tartane had drifted to her destruction. Anchoring outside the hay, Captain Beresford sent the first lieutenant, Mr. Bullock, in the long-boat, with Arthur and a well-armed force, with instructions to offer no violence, but to reconnoitre; and if they found Mademoiselle de Bourke, or any others of the party, to do their best for their release by promises of ransom or representations of the consequences of detaining them. Arthur was prepared to offer his own piastres at once in case of need of immediate payment. He was by this time tolerably versed in the vernacular of the Mediterranean, and a cook's boy, shipped at Gibraltar, was also supposed to be capable of interpreting.

The beautiful bay, almost realising the description of Æneas' landing-place, lay before them, the still green waters within reflecting the fantastic rocks and the wreaths of verdure which crowned them, while the white mountain-tops rose like clouds in the far distance against the azure sky. Arthur could only, however, think of all this fair scene as a cruel prison, and those sharp rocks as the jaws of a trap, when he saw the ribs of the tartane still jammed into the rock where she had struck, and where he had saved the two children as they were washed up the hatchway. He saw the rock where the other three had clung, and where he had left the little girl. He remembered the crowd of howling, yelling savages, leaping and gesticulating on the beach, and his heart trembled as he wondered how it had ended.

Where were the Cabeleyzes who had thus greeted them? The bay seemed perfectly lonely. Not a sound was to be heard but the regular dip of the oars, the cry of a startled bird, and the splash of a flock of seals, which had been sunning themselves on the shore, and which floundered into the sea like Proteus' flock of yore before Ulysses. Would that Proteus himself had still been there to be captured and interrogated! For the place was so entirely deserted that, saving for the remains of the wreck, he must have believed himself mistaken in the locality, and the lieutenant began to question him whether it had been daylight when he came ashore.

Could the natives have hidden themselves at sight of an armed vessel? Mr. Bullock resolved on landing, very cautiously, and with a sufficient guard. On the shore some fragments of broken boxes and packing cases appeared; and a sailor pointed out the European lettering painted on one—sse de B–. It plainly was part of the address to the Comtesse de Bourke. This encouraged the party in their search. They ascended the path which poor Hébert and Lanty Callaghan had so often painfully climbed, and found themselves before the square of reed hovels, also deserted, but with black marks where fires had been lighted, and with traces of recent habitation.

Arthur picked up a rag of the Bourke livery, and another of a brocade which he had seen the poor Countess wearing. Was this all the relic that he should ever be able to take to her husband?

He peered about anxiously in hopes of discovering further tokens, and Mr. Bullock was becoming impatient of his lingering, when suddenly his eye was struck by a score on the bark of a chestnut tree like a cross, cut with a feeble hand. Beneath, close to the trunk, was a stone, beyond the corner of which appeared a bit of paper. He pounced upon it. It was the title-page of Estelle's precious Télémaque, and on the back was written in French, If any good Christian ever finds this, I pray him to carry it to M. the French Consul at Algiers. We are five poor prisoners, the Abbé de St. Eudoce, Estelle, daughter of the Comte de Bourke, and our servants, Jacques Hébert, Laurent Callaghan, Victorine Renouf. The Cabeleyzes are taking us away to their mountains. We are in slavery, in hunger, filth, and deprivation of all things. We pray day and night that the good God will send some one to rescue us, for we are in great misery, and they persecute us to make us deny our faith. O, whoever you may be, come and deliver us while we are yet alive.'

Arthur was almost choked with tears as he translated this piteous letter to the lieutenant, and recollected the engaging, enthusiastic little maiden, as he had seen her on the Rhone, but now brought to such a state. He implored Mr. Bullock to pursue the track up the mountain, and was grieved at this being treated as absurdly impossible, but then recollecting himself, 'You could not, sir, but I might follow her and make them understand that she must be saved —'

'And give them another captive,' said Bullock; 'I thought you had had enough of that. You will do more good to this flame of yours—'

'No flame, sir. She is a mere child, little older than her brother. But she must not remain among these lawless savages.'

'No! But we don't throw the helve after the hatchet, my lad! All you can do is to take this epistle to the French Consul, who might find it hard to understand without your explanations. At any rate, my orders are to bring you safe on board again.'

Arthur had no choice but to submit, and Captain Beresford, who had a wife and children at home, was greatly touched by the sight of the childish writing of the poor little motherless girl; above all when Arthur explained that the high-sounding title of Abbé de St. Eudoce only meant one who was more likely to be a charge than a help to her.

France was for the nonce allied with England, and the dread of passing to Sweden through British seas had apparently been quite futile, since, if Captain Beresford recollected the Irish blood of the Count, it was only as an additional cause for taking interest in him. Towards the Moorish pirates the interest of the two nations united them. It was intolerable to think of the condition of the captives; and the captain, anxious to lose no time, rejoiced that his orders were such as to justify him in sailing at once for Algiers to take effectual measures with the consul before letting the family know the situation of the poor Demoiselle de Bourke.

CHAPTER XI—THE PIRATE CITY

'With dazed vision unawares
From the long alley's latticed shade
Emerged, I came upon the great
Pavilion of the Caliphat.
Right to the carven cedarn doors,
Flung inward over spangled floors,
Broad-based flights of marble stairs
Ran up with golden balustrade,
    After the fashion of the time,
    And humour of the golden prime
    Of good Haroun Alraschid.'

TENNYSON.

Civilised and innocuous existence has no doubt been a blessing to Algiers as well as to the entire Mediterranean, but it has not improved the picturesqueness of its aspect any more than the wild and splendid 'tiger, tiger burning bright,' would be more ornamental with his claws pared, the fiery gleam of his yellow eyes quenched, and his spirit tamed, so as to render him only an exaggerated domestic cat. The steamer, whether of peace or war, is a melancholy substitute for the splendid though sinister galley, with her ranks of oars and towers of canvas, or for the dainty lateen-sailed vessels, skimming the waters like flying fish, and the Frank garb ill replaces the graceful Arab dress. The Paris-like block of houses ill replaces the graceful Moorish architecture, undisturbed when the *Calypso* sailed into the harbour, and the amphitheatre-like city rose before her, in successive terraces of dazzling white, interspersed with palms and other trees here and there, with mosques and minarets rising above them, and with a crown of strong fortifications. The harbour itself was protected by a strongly-fortified mole, and some parley passed with the governor of the strong and grim-looking castle adjacent—a huge round tower erected by the Spaniards, and showing three ranks of brazen teeth in the shape of guns.

Finally, the Algerines having been recently brought to their bearings, as Captain Beresford said, entrance was permitted, and the *Calypso* enjoyed the shelter of the mole; while he, in full-dress uniform, took boat and went ashore, and with him the two escaped prisoners. Fareek remained on board till the English Consul could be consulted on his fate.

115

England and France were on curious terms with Algiers. The French had bombarded the city in 1686, and had obtained a treaty by which a consul constantly resided in the city, and the persons and property of French subjects were secured from piracy, or if captured were always released. The English had made use of the possession of Gibraltar and Minorca to enforce a like treaty. There was a little colony of European merchants—English, French, and Dutch—in the lower town, near the harbour, above which the Arab town rose, as it still rises, in a steep stair. Ships of all these nations traded at the port, and quite recently the English Consul, Thomas Thompson by name, had vindicated the honour of his flag by citing before the Dey a man who had insulted him on the narrow causeway of the mole. The Moor was sentenced to receive 2200 strokes of bastinado on the feet, 1000 the first day, 1200 on the second, and he died in consequence, so that Englishmen safely walked the narrow streets. The Dey who had inflicted this punishment was, however, lately dead. Mehemed had been elected and installed by the chief Janissaries, and it remained to be proved whether he would show himself equally anxious to be on good terms with the Christian Powers.

Arthur's heart had learnt to beat at sight of the British ensign with emotions very unlike those with which he had seen it wave at Sheriffmuir; but it looked strange above the low walls of a Moorish house, plain outside, but with a richly cusped and painted horse-shoe arch at the entrance to a lovely cloistered court, with a sparkling fountain surrounded by orange trees with fruit of all shades from green to gold. Servants in white garments and scarlet fezzes, black, brown, or white (by courtesy), seemed to swarm in all directions; and one of them called a youth in European garb, but equally dark-faced with the rest, and not too good an English scholar. However, he conducted them through a still more beautiful court, lined with brilliant mosaics in the spandrels of the exquisite arches supported on slender shining marble columns.

Mr. Thompson's English coat and hearty English face looked incongruous, as at sight of the blue and white uniform he came forward with all the hospitable courtesy due to a post-captain. There was shaking of hands, and doffing of cocked hats, and calling for wine, and pipes, and coffee, in the Alhambra-like hall, where a table covered with papers tied with red tape, in front of a homely leathern chair, looked more homelike than suitable. Other chairs there were for Frank guests, who preferred them to the divan and piles of cushions on which the Moors transacted business.

'What can I do for you, sir?' he asked of the captain, 'or for this little master,' he added, looking at Ulysse, who was standing by Arthur. 'He is serving the King early.'

'I don't belong to your King George,' broke out the young gentleman. 'He is an *usurpateur*. I have only this uniform on till I can get my proper clothes. I am the son of the Comte de Bourke, Ambassador to Spain and Sweden. I serve no one but King Louis!'

'That is plain to be seen!' said Mr. Thompson. 'The Gallic cock crows early. But is he indeed the son of Count Bourke, about whom the French Consul has been in such trouble?'

'Even so, sir,' replied the captain. 'I am come to ask you to present him, with this gentleman, Mr. Hope, to your French colleague. Mr. Hope, to whom the child's life and liberty are alike owing, has information to give which may lead to the rescue of the boy's sister and uncle with their servants.'

Mr. Thompson had heard of a Moorish galley coming in with an account of having lost a Genoese prize, with ladies on board, in the late storm. He was sure that the tidings Mr. Hope brought would be most welcome, but he knew that the French Consul was gone up with a distinguished visitor, M. Dessault, for an audience of the Dey; and, in the meantime, his guests must dine with him. And Arthur narrated his adventures.

The Consul shook his head when he heard of Djigheli Bay.

'Those fellows, the Cabeleyzes, hate the French, and make little enough of the Dey, though they do send home Moors who fall into their hands. Did you see a ruined fort on a promontory? That was the Bastion de France. The old King Louis put it up and garrisoned it, but these rogues contrived a surprise, and made four hundred prisoners, and ever since they have been neither to have nor to hold. Well for you, young gentleman, that you did not fall into their hands, but those of the country Moors—very decent folk—descended, they say, from the Spanish Moors. A renegade got you off, did he? Yes, they will sometimes do that, though at an awful risk. If they are caught, they are hung up alive on hooks to the walls. You had an escape, I can tell you, and so had he, poor fellow, of being taken alive.'

'He knew the risk!' said Arthur, in a low voice; 'but my mother had once been good to him, and he dared everything for me.'

The Consul readily estimated Arthur's legacy as amounting to little less than £200, and was also ready to give him bills of exchange for it. The next question was as to Fareek. To return him to his own country was impossible; and though the Consul offered to buy him of Arthur, not only did the young Scot revolt at the idea of making traffic of the faithful fellow, but Mr. Thompson owned that there might be some risk in Algiers of his being recognised as a runaway; and though this was very slight, it was better not to give any cause of offence. Captain Beresford thought the poor man might be disposed of at Port Mahon, and Arthur kept to himself that Tam's bequest was sacred to him. His next wish was for clothes to which he might have a better right than to the uniform of the senior midshipman of H.M.S. *Calypso*—a garb in which he did not like to appear before the French Consul. Mr. Thompson consulted his Greek clerk, and a chest belonging to a captured merchantman, which had been claimed as British property, but had not found an owner, was opened, and proved to contain a wardrobe sufficient to equip Arthur like other gentlemen of the day, in a dark crimson coat, with a little gold lace about it, and the rest of the dress white, a wide beaver hat, looped up with a rosette, and everything, indeed, except shoes, and he was obliged to retain those of the senior midshipman. With his dark hair tied back, and a suspicion of powder, he found himself more like the youth whom Lady Nithsdale had introduced in Madame de Varennes' *salon* than he had felt for the last month; and, moreover, his shyness and awkwardness had in great measure disappeared during his vicissitudes, and he had made many steps towards manhood.

Ulysse had in the meantime been consigned to a kind, motherly, portly Mrs. Thompson, who, accustomed as she was to hearing of strange adventures, was aghast at what the child had undergone, and was enchanted with the little French gentleman who spoke English so well, and to whom his Grand Seigneur airs returned by instinct in contact with a European lady; but his eye instantly sought Arthur, nor would he be content without a seat next to his protector at the dinner, early as were all dinners then, and a compound of Eastern and Western dishes, the latter very welcome to the travellers, and affording the Consul's wife themes of discourse on her difficulties in compounding them.

Pipes, siesta, and coffee followed, Mr. Thompson assuring them that his French colleague would not be ready to receive them till after the like repose had been undergone, and that he had already sent a billet to announce their coming.

The French Consulate was not distant. The *fleur-de-lis* waved over a house similar to Mr. Thompson's, but they were admitted with greater ceremony, when Mr. Thompson at length conducted them. Servants and slaves, brown and black, clad in white with blue sashes, and white officials in blue liveries, were drawn up in the first court in two lines to receive them; and the Chevalier, taking it all to himself, paraded in front with the utmost grandeur, until, at the next archway, two gentlemen, resplendent in gold lace, came forward with low bows. At sight of the little fellow there were cries of joy. M. Dessault spread out his arms, clasped the child to his breast, and shed tears over him, so that the less emotional Englishmen thought at first that they must be kinsmen. However, Arthur came in for a like embrace as the boy's preserver; and if Captain Beresford had not stepped back and looked uncomprehending and rigid he might have come in for the same.

Seated in the verandah, Arthur told his tale and presented the letter, over which there were more tears, as, indeed, well there might be over the condition of the little girl and her simple mode of describing it. It was nearly a month since the corsair had arrived, and the story of the Genoese tartane being captured and lost with French ladies on board had leaked out. The French Consul had himself seen and interrogated the Dutch renegade captain, had become convinced of the identity of the unfortunate passengers, and had given up all hopes of them, so that he greeted the boy as one risen from the dead.

To know that the boy's sister and uncle were still in the hands of the Cabeleyzes was almost worse news than the death of his mother, for this wild Arab tribe had a terrible reputation even among the Moors and Turks.

The only thing that could be devised after consultation between the two consuls, the French envoy, and the English captain, was that an audience should be demanded of the Dey, and Estelle's letter presented the next morning. Meanwhile Arthur and Ulysse were to remain as guests at the English Consulate. The French one would have made them welcome, but there was no lady in his house; and Mrs. Thompson had given Arthur a hint that his little charge would be the better for womanly care.

There was further consultation whether young Hope, as a runaway slave—who had, however, carried off a relapsed renegade with him—would be safe on shore beyond the precincts of the Consulate; but as no one had any claim on him, and it might be desirable to have his evidence at hand, it was thought safe that he should remain, and Captain Beresford promised to come ashore in the morning to join the petitioners to the Dey.

Perhaps he was not sorry, any more than was Arthur, for the opportunity of beholding the wonderful city and palace, which were like a dream of beauty. He came ashore early, with two or three officers, all in full uniform; and the audience having been granted, the whole party—consuls, M. Dessault, and their attendants—mounted the steep, narrow stone steps leading up the hill between the walls of houses with fantastically carved doorways or lattices; while bare-legged Arabs niched themselves into every coigne of vantage with baskets of fruit or eggs, or else embroidering pillows and slippers with exquisite taste.

The beauty of the buildings was unspeakable, and they projected enough to make a cool shade—only a narrow fragment of deep blue sky being visible above them. The party did not, however, ascend the whole 497 steps, as the abode of the Dey was then not the citadel, but the palace of Djenina in the heart of the city. Turning aside, they made their way thither over terraces partly in the rock, partly on the roofs of houses.

Fierce-looking Janissaries, splendidly equipped, guarded the entrance, with an air so proud and consequential as to remind Arthur of poor Yusuf's assurances of the magnificence that might await little Ulysse as an Aga of that corps. Even as they admitted the infidels they looked defiance at them from under the manifold snowy folds of their mighty turbans.

If the beauty of the consuls' houses had struck and startled Arthur, far more did the region into which he was now admitted seem like a dream of fairyland as he passed through ranks of orange trees round sparkling fountains—worthy of Versailles itself—courts surrounded with cloisters, sparkling with priceless mosaics, in those brilliant colours which Eastern taste alone can combine so as to avoid gaudiness, arches and columns of ineffable grace and richness, halls with domes emulating the sky, or else ceiled with white marble lacework, whose tracery seemed delicate and varied as the richest Venice point! But the wonderful beauty seemed to him to have in it something terrible and weird, like that fairyland of his native country, whose glory and charm is overshadowed by the knowledge of the teinds to be paid to hell. It was an unnatural, incomprehensible world; and from longing to admire and examine, he only wished to be out of it, felt it a relief to fix his eyes upon the uniforms of the captain and the consuls, and did not wonder that Ulysse, instead of proudly heading the procession, shrank up to him and clasped his hand as his protector.

The human figures were as strange as the architecture; the glittering of Janissaries in the outer court, which seemed a sort of guardroom, the lines of those on duty in the next, and in the third court the black slaves in white garments, enhancing the blackness of their limbs, each with a formidable curved scimitar. At the golden cusped archway beyond, all had to remove their shoes as though entering a mosque. The Consuls bade the new-comers submit to this, adding that it was only since the recent victory that it had not been needful to lay aside the sword on entering the Dey's august presence. The chamber seemed to the eyes of the strangers one web of magic splendour —gold-crusted lacework above, arches on one side open to a beauteous garden, and opposite semicircles of richly-robed Janissary officers, all culminating in a dazzling throne, where sat a white-turbaned figure, before whom the visitors all had to bow lower than European independence could well brook.

The Dey's features were not very distinctly seen at the distance where etiquette required them to stand; but Arthur thought him hardly worthy to be master of such fine-looking beings as Abou Ben Zegri and many others of the Moors, being in fact a little sturdy Turk, with Tartar features, not nearly so graceful as the Moors and Arabs, nor so handsome and imposing as the Janissaries of Circassian blood. Turkish was the court language; and even if he understood any other, an interpreter was a necessary part of the etiquette. M. Dessault instructed the interpreter, who understood with a readiness which betrayed that he was one of the many renegades in the Algerine service.

The Dey was too dignified to betray much emotion; but he spoke a few words, and these were understood to profess his willingness to assist in the matter. A richly-clad official, who was, Mr. Thompson whispered, a Secretary of State, came to attend the party in a smaller but equally beautiful room, where pipes and coffee were served, and a consultation took place with the two Consuls, which was, of course, incomprehensible to the anxious listeners. M. Dessault's interest was deeply concerned in the matter, since he was a connection of the Varennes family, to which poor Madame de Bourke belonged.

Commands from the Dey, it was presently explained, would be utterly disregarded by these wild mountaineers—nay, would probably lead to the murder of the captives in defiance. But it was known that if these wild beings paid deference to any one, it was to the Grand Marabout at Bugia; and the Secretary promised to send a letter in the Dey's name, which, with a considerable present, might induce him to undertake the negotiation. Therewith the audience terminated, after M. Dessault had laid a splendid diamond snuff-box at the feet of the Secretary.

The Consuls were somewhat disgusted at the notion of having recourse to the Marabouts, whom the French Consul called *vilains charlatan*, and the English one filthy scoundrels and impostors. Like the Indian Fakirs, opined Captain Beresford; like the begging friars, said M. Dessault, and to this the Consuls assented. Just, however, as the Dominicans, besides the low class of barefooted friars, had a learned and cultivated set of brethren in high repute at the Universities, and a general at Rome, so it appeared that the Marabouts, besides their wild crew of masterful beggars, living at free quarters, partly through pretended sanctity, partly through the awe inspired by cabalistic arts, had a higher class who dwelt in cities, and were highly esteemed, for the sake of either ten years' abstinence from food or the attainment of fifty sciences, by one or other of which means an angelic nature was held to be attained.

Fifty sciences! This greatly astonished the strangers, but they were told by the residents that all the knowledge of the highly cultivated Arabs of Bagdad and the Moors of Spain had been handed on to the select few of their African descendants, and that really beautiful poetry was still produced by the Marabouts. Certainly no one present could doubt of the architectural skill and taste of the Algerines, and Mr. Thompson declared that not a tithe of the wonders of their mechanical art had been seen, describing the wonderful silver tree of Tlemcen, covered with birds, who, by the action of wind, were made to produce the songs of each different species which they represented, till a falcon on the topmost branch uttered a harsh cry, and all became silent. General education had, however, fallen to a low ebb among the population, and the wisdom of the ancients was chiefly concentrated among the higher class of Marabouts, whose headquarters were at Bugia, and their present chief, Hadji Eseb Ben Hassan, had the reputation of a saint, which the Consuls believed to be well founded.

The Cabeleyzes, though most irregular Moslems, were extremely superstitious as regarded the supernatural arts supposed to be possessed by the Marabouts, and if these could be induced to take up the cause of the prisoners, there would be at least some chance of their success.

And not long after the party had arrived at the French Consulate, where they were to dine, a messenger arrived with a parcel rolled up in silk, embroidered with gold, and containing a strip of paper beautifully emblazoned, and in Turkish characters. The Consul read it, and found it to be a really strong recommendation to the Marabout to do his utmost for the servants of the Dey's brother, the King of France, now in the hands of the children of Shaitan.

'Well purchased,' said M. Dessault; 'though that snuff-box came from the hands of the Elector of Bavaria!'

As soon as the meal was over, the French Consul, instead of taking his siesta as usual, began to take measures for chartering a French tartane to go to Bugia immediately. He found there was great interest excited, not only among the Christian merchants, but among Turks, Moors, and Jews, so horrible was the idea of captivity among the Cabeleyzes. The Dey set the example of sending down five purses of sequins towards the young lady's ransom, and many more contributions came in unasked. It was true that the bearers expected no small consideration in return, but this was willingly given, and the feeling manifested was a perfect astonishment to all the friends at the Consulate.

The French national interpreter, Ibrahim Aga, was charged with the negotiations with the Marabout. Arthur entreated to go with him, and with some hesitation this was agreed to, since the sight of an old friend might be needed to reassure any survivors of the poor captives—for it was hardly thought possible that all could still survive the hardships of the mountains in the depth of winter, even if they were spared by the ferocity of their captors.

Ulysse, the little son and heir, was not to be exposed to the perils of the seas till his sister's fate was decided, and accordingly he was to remain under the care of Mrs. Thompson; while Captain Beresford meant to cruise about in the neighbourhood, having a great desire to know the result of the enterprise, and hoping also that if Mademoiselle de Bourke still lived he might be permitted to restore her to her relations. Letters, clothes, and comforts were provided, and placed under the charge of the interpreter and of Arthur, together with a considerable gratuity for the Marabout, and authority for any ransom that Cabeleyze rapacity might require,—still, however, with great doubt whether all might not be too late.

CHAPTER XII—ON THE MOUNTAINS

'We cannot miss him. He doth make our fire,
Fetch in our wood, and serve in offices
That profit us.'

Tempest.

Bugia, though midway on the 'European lake,' is almost unknown to modern travellers, though it has become a French possession.

It looked extremely beautiful when the French tartane entered it, rising from the sea like a magnificent amphitheatre, at the foot of the mountains that circled round it, and guarded by stern battlemented castles, while the arches of one of the great old Roman aqueducts made a noble cord to the arc described by the lower part of the town.

The harbour, a finer one naturally than that of Algiers, contained numerous tartanes and other vessels, for, as Ibrahim Aga, who could talk French very well, informed Arthur, the inhabitants were good workers in iron, and drove a trade in plough-shares and other implements, besides wax and oil. But it was no resort of Franks, and he insisted that Arthur should only come on shore in a Moorish dress, which had been provided at Algiers. Thanks to young Hope's naturally dark complexion, and the exposure of the last month, he might very well pass for a Moor: and he had learnt to wear the white caftan, wide trousers, broad sash, and scarlet fez, circled with muslin, so naturally that he was not likely to be noticed as a European.

The city, in spite of its external beauty, proved to be ruinous within, and in the midst of the Moorish houses and courts still were visible remnants of the old Roman town that had in past ages flourished there. Like Algiers, it had narrow climbing streets, excluding sunshine, and through these the guide Ibrahim had secured led the way; while in single file came the interpreter, Arthur, two black slaves bearing presents for the Marabout, and four men besides as escort. Once or twice there was a vista down a broader space, with an awning over it, where selling and buying were going on, always of some single species of merchandise.

Thus they arrived at one of those Moorish houses, to whose beauty Arthur was becoming accustomed. It had, however, a less luxurious and grave aspect than the palaces of Algiers, and the green colour sacred to the Prophet prevailed in the inlaid work, which Ibrahim Aga told him consisted chiefly of maxims from the Koran.

No soldiers were on guard, but there were a good many young men wholly clad in white—neophytes endeavouring to study the fifty sciences, mostly sitting on the ground, writing copies, either of the sacred books, or of the treatises on science and medicine which had descended from time almost immemorial; all rehearsed aloud what they learnt or wrote, so as to produce a strange hum. A grave official, similarly clad, but with a green sash, came to meet them, and told them that the chief Marabout was sick; but on hearing from the interpreter that they were bearers of a letter from the Dey, he went back with the intelligence, and presently returned salaaming very low, to introduce them to another of the large halls with lacework ceilings, where it was explained that the Grand Marabout was, who was suffering from ague. The fit was passing off, and he would be able to attend of the coffee and the pipes which were presented to his honoured guests so soon as they had partaken them.

After a delay, very trying to Arthur's anxiety, though beguiled by such coffee and tobacco as he was never likely to encounter again, Hadji Eseb Ben Hassan, a venerable-looking man, appeared, with a fine white beard and keen eyes, slenderly formed, and with an air of very considerable ability—much more so than the Dey, in all his glittering splendour of gold, jewels, and embroidery, whereas this old man wore the pure white woollen garments of the Moor, with the green sash, and an emerald to fasten the folds of his white turban.

Ibrahim Aga prostrated himself as if before the Dey, and laid before the Marabout, as a first gift, a gold watch; then, after a blessing had been given in return, he produced with great ceremony the Dey's letter, to which every one in the apartment did obeisance by touching the floor with their foreheads, and the Grand Marabout further rubbed it on his brow before proceeding to read it, which he chose to do for himself, chanting it out in a low, humming voice. It was only a recommendation, and the other letter was from the French Consul containing all particulars. The Marabout seemed much startled, and interrogated the interpreter. Arthur could follow them in some degree, and presently the keen eye of the old man seemed to detect his interest, for there was a pointing to him, an explanation that he had been there, and presently Hadji Eseb addressed a question to him in the vernacular Arabic. He understood and answered, but the imperfect language or his looks betrayed him, for Hadji Eseb demanded, 'Thou art Frank, my son?'

Ibrahim Aga, mortally afraid of the consequences of having brought a disguised Giaour into these sacred precincts, began what Arthur perceived to be a lying assurance of his having embraced Islam; and he was on the point of breaking in upon the speech, when the Marabout observed his gesture, and said gravely, 'My son, falsehood is not needed to shield a brave Christian; a faithful worshipper of Issa Ben Mariam receives honour if he does justice and works righteousness according to his own creed, even though he be blind to the true faith. Is it true, good youth, that thou art—not as this man would have me believe—one of the crew from Algiers, but art come to strive for the release of thy sister?'

Arthur gave the history as best he could, for his month's practice had made him able to speak the vernacular so as to be fairly comprehensible, and the Marabout, who was evidently a man of very high abilities, often met him half way, and suggested the word at which he stumbled. He was greatly touched by the account, even in the imperfect manner in which the youth could give it; and there was no doubt that he was a man of enlarged mind and beneficence, who had not only mastered the fifty sciences, but had seen something of the world.

He had not only made his pilgrimage to Mecca more than once, but had been at Constantinople, and likewise at Tunis and Tripoli; thus, with powers both acute and awake, he understood more than his countrymen of European Powers and their relation to one another. As a civilised and cultivated man, he was horrified at the notion of the tenderly-nurtured child being in the clutches of savages like the Cabeleyzes; but the first difficulty was to find out where she was; for, as he said, pointing towards the mountains, they were a wide space, and it would be hunting a partridge on the hills.

Looking at his chief councillor, Azim Reverdi, he demanded whether some of the wanderers of their order, whom he named, could not be sent through the mountains to discover where any such prisoners might be; but after going into the court in quest of these persons, Azim returned with tidings that a Turkish soldier had returned on the previous day to the town, and had mentioned that on Mount Couco, Sheyk Abderrahman was almost at war with his subordinates, Eyoub and Ben Yakoub, about some shipwrecked Frank captives, if they had not already settled the matter by murdering them all, and, as was well known, nothing would persuade this ignorant, lawless tribe that nothing was more abhorrent to the Prophet than human sacrifices.

Azim had already sent two disciples to summon the Turk to the presence of the Grand Marabout, and in due time he appeared—a rough, heavy, truculent fellow enough, but making awkward salaams as one in great awe of the presence in which he stood—unwilling awe perhaps—full of superstitious fear tempered by pride—for the haughty Turks revolted against homage to one of the subject race of Moors.

His language was only now and then comprehensible to Arthur, but Ibrahim kept up a running translation into French for his benefit.

There were captives—infidels—saved from the wreck, he knew not how many, but he was sure of one—a little maid with hair like the unwound cocoon, so that they called her the Daughter of the Silkworm. It was about her that the chief struggle was. She had fallen to the lot of Ben Yakoub, who had been chestnut-gathering by the sea at the time of the wreck; but when he arrived on Mount Couco the Sheyk Abderrahman had claimed her and hers as the head of the tribe, and had carried her off to his own adowara in the valley of Ein Gebel.

The Turk, Murad, had been induced by Yakoub to join him and sixteen more armed men whom he had got together to demand her. For it was he who had rescued her from the waves, carried her up the mountains, fed her all this time, and he would not have her snatched away from him, though for his part Murad thought it would have been well to be quit of them, for not only were they Giaours, but he verily believed them to be of the race of Jinns. The little fair-haired maid had papers with strange signs on them. She wrote—actually wrote—a thing that he believed no Sultana Velidè even had ever been known to do at Stamboul. Moreover, she twisted strings about on her hands in a manner that was fearful to look at. It was said to be only to amuse the children, but for his part he believed it was for some evil spell. What was certain was that the other, a woman full grown, could, whenever any one offended her, raise a Jinn in a cloud of smoke, which caused such sneezing that she was lost sight of. And yet these creatures had so bewitched their captors that there were like to be hard blows before they were disposed of, unless his advice were taken to make an end of them altogether. Indeed, two of the men, the mad Santon and the chief slave, had been taken behind a bush to be sacrificed, when the Daughter of the Silkworm came between with her incantations, and fear came upon Sheyk Yakoub. Murad evidently thought it highly advisable that the chief Marabout should intervene to put a stop to these doings, and counteract the mysterious influence exercised by these strange beings.

High time, truly, Arthur and Ibrahim Aga likewise felt it, to go to the rescue, since terror and jealousy might, it appeared, at any time impel *ces barbares féroces*, as Ibrahim called them, to slaughter their prisoners. To their great joy, the Marabout proved to be of the same opinion, in spite of his sickness, which, being an intermitting ague, would leave him free for a couple of days, and might be driven off by the mountain air. He promised to set forth early the next day, and kept the young man and the interpreter as his guests for the night, Ibrahim going first on board to fetch the parcel of clothes and provisions which M. Dessault had sent for the Abbé and Mademoiselle de

Bourke, and for an instalment of the ransom, which the Hadji Eseb assured him might safely be carried under his own sacred protection.

Arthur did not see much of his host, who seemed to be very busy consulting with his second in command on the preparations, for probably the expedition was a delicate undertaking, even for him, and his companions had to be carefully chosen.

Ibrahim had advised Arthur to stay quietly where he was, and not venture into the city, and he spent his time as he best might by the help of a *narghilé*, which was hospitably presented to him, though the strictness of Marabout life forbade the use alike of tobacco and coffee.

Before dawn the courts of the house were astir. Mules, handsomely trapped, were provided to carry the principal persons of the party wherever it might be possible, and there were some spare ones, ridden at first by inferiors, but intended for the captives, should they be recovered.

It was very cold, being the last week in November, and all were wrapped in heavy woollen haiks over their white garments, except one wild-looking fellow, whose legs and arms were bare, and who only seemed to possess one garment of coarse dark sackcloth. He skipped and ran by the side of the mules, chanting and muttering, and Ibrahim observed in French that he was one of the Sunakites, or fanatic Marabouts, and advised Arthur to beware of him; but, though dangerous in himself, his presence would be a sufficient protection from all other thieves or vagabonds. Indeed, Arthur saw the fellow glaring unpleasantly at him, when the sun summoned all the rest to their morning devotions. He was glad that he had made the fact of his Christianity known, for he could no more act Moslem than *be* one, and Hadji Eseb kept the Sunakite in check by a stern glance, so that no harm ensued.

Afterwards Arthur was bidden to ride near the chief, who talked a good deal, asking intelligent questions. Gibraltar had impressed him greatly, and it also appeared that in one of his pilgrimages the merchant vessel he was in had been rescued from some Albanian pirates by an English ship, which held the Turks as allies, and thus saved them from undergoing vengeance for the sufferings of the Greeks. Thus the good old man felt that he owed a debt of gratitude which Allah required him to pay, even to the infidel.

Up steep roads the mules climbed. The first night the halt was at a Cabyle village, where hospitality was eagerly offered to persons of such high reputation for sanctity as the Marabouts; but afterwards habitations grew more scanty as the ground rose higher, and there was no choice but to encamp in the tents brought by the attendants, and which seemed to Arthur a good exchange for the dirty Cabyle huts.

Altogether the journey took six days. The mules climbed along wild paths on the verge of giddy precipices, where even on foot Arthur would have hesitated to venture. The scenery would now be thought magnificent, but it was simply frightful to the mind of the early eighteenth century, especially when a constant watch had to be kept to avoid the rush of stones, or avalanches, on an almost imperceptible, nearly perpendicular path, where it was needful to trust to the guidance of the Sunakite, the only one of the cavalcade who had been there before.

On the last day they found themselves on the borders of a slope of pines and other mountain-growing trees, bordering a wide valley or ravine where the Sunakite hinted that Abderrahman might be found.

The cavalcade pursued a path slightly indicated by the treading of feet and hoofs, and presently there emerged on them from a slighter side track between the red stems of the great pines a figure nearly bent double under the weight of two huge faggots, with a basket of great solid fir-cones on the top of them. Very scanty garments seemed to be vouchsafed to him, and the bare arms and legs were so white, as well as of a length so unusual among Arabs or Moors, that simultaneously the Marabout exclaimed, 'One of the Giaour captives,' and Arthur cried out, 'La Jeunesse! Laurence!'

There was only just time for a start and a response, 'M. Arture! And is it yourself?' before a howl of vituperation was heard—of abuse of all the ancestry of the cur of an infidel slave, the father of tardiness—and a savage-looking man appeared, brandishing a cudgel, with which he was about to belabour his unfortunate slave, when he was arrested by astonishment, and perhaps terror, at the goodly company of Marabouts. Hadji Eseb entered into conversation with him, and meanwhile Lanty broke forth, 'O wirrah, wirrah, Master Arthur! an' have they made a haythen Moor of ye? By the powers, but this is worse than all. What will Mademoiselle say?—she that has held up the faith of every one of us, like a little saint and martyr as she is! Though, to be sure, ye are but a Protestant; only these folks don't know the differ.'

'If you would let me speak, Laurence,' said Arthur, 'you would hear that I am no more a Moslem than yourself, only my Frank dress might lead to trouble. We are come to deliver you all, with a ransom from the French Consul. Are you all safe—Mademoiselle and all? and how many of you?'

'Mademoiselle and M. l'Abbé were safe and well three days since,' said Lanty; 'but that spalpeen there is my master and poor Victorine's, and will not let us put a foot near them.'

'Where are they? How many?' anxiously asked Arthur.

'There are five of us altogether,' said Lanty; 'praise be to Him who has saved us thus far. We know the touch of cold steel at our throats, as well as ever I knew the poor misthress' handbell; and unless our Lady, and St. Lawrence, and the rest of them, keep the better watch on us, the rascals will only ransom us without our heads, so jealous and bloodthirsty they are. The Bey of Constantina sent for us once, but all we got by that was worse usage than the very dogs in Paris, and being dragged up these weary hills, where Maître Hubert and I carried Mademoiselle every foot of the way on our backs, and she begging our pardon so prettily—only she could not walk, the rocks had so bruised her darlin' little feet.'

'This is their chief holy man, Lanty. If any one can prevail on these savages to release you it is he.'

'And how come you to be hand and glove with them, Masther Arthur—you that I thought drownded with poor Madame and the little Chevalier and the rest?'

'The Chevalier is not drowned, Laurent. He is safe in the Consul's house at Algiers.'

'Now heaven and all the saints be praised! The Chevalier safe and well! 'Tis a very miracle!' cried Lanty, letting fall his burthen, as he clasped his hands in ecstasy and performed a caper which, in spite of all his master Eyoub's respect for the Marabouts, brought a furious yell of rage, and a tremendous blow with the cudgel, which Lanty, in his joy, seemed to receive as if it had been a feather.

Hadji Eseb averted a further blow; and understanding from Arthur that the poor fellow's transport was caused by the tidings of the safety of his master's son, he seemed touched, and bade that he and Eyoub should lead the way to the place of durance of the chief prisoners. On the way Ibrahim Aga interrogated both Eyoub in vernacular Arabic and Lanty in French. The former was sullen, only speaking from his evident awe of the Marabouts, the latter voluble with joy and hope.

Arthur learnt that the letter he had found under the stone was the fourth that Estelle and Hébert had written. There had been a terrible journey up the mountains, when Lanty had fully thought Victorine must close her sufferings in some frightful ravine; but, nevertheless, she had recovered health and strength with every day's ascent above the close, narrow valley. They were guarded all the way by Arabs armed to the teeth to prevent a rescue by the Bey of Constantina.

On their arrival at the valley, which was the headquarters of the tribe, the sheyk of the entire clan had laid claim to the principal captives, and had carried off the young lady and her uncle; and in his dwelling she had a boarded floor to sleep on, and had been made much more comfortable than in the squalid huts below. Her original master, Yakoub, had, however, come to seize her, with the force described by Murad. Then it was that again there was a threat to kill rather than resign them; but on this occasion it was averted by Sheyk Abderrahman's son, a boy of about fourteen, who threw himself on his knees before Mademoiselle, and prayed his father earnestly for her life.

'They spared her then,' said Lanty, 'and, mayhap, worse still may come of that. Yakoub, the villain, ended by getting her back till they can have a council of their tribe, and there she is in his filthy hut; but the gossoon, Selim, as they call him, prowls about the place as if he were bewitched. All the children are, for that matter, wherever she goes. She makes cats' cradles for them, and sings to them, and tells them stories in her own sweet way out of the sacred history—such as may bring her into trouble one of these days. Maître Hébert heard her one day telling them the story of Moses, and he warned her that if she went on in that fashion it might be the death of us all. "But," says she, "suppose we made Selim, and little Zuleika, and all the rest of them, Christians? Suppose we brought all the tribe to come down and ask baptism, like as St. Nona did in the *Lives of the Saints*?" He told her it was more like that they would only get her darling little head cut off, if no worse, but he could not get her to think that mattered at all at all. She would have a crown and a palm up in heaven, and after her name in the Calendar on earth, bless her.'

Then he went on to tell that Yakoub was furious at the notion of resigning his prize, and (Agamemnon-like) declared that if she were taken from him he should demand Victorine from Eyoub. Unfortunately she was recovering her good looks in the mountain air; and, worse still, the spring of her 'blessed little Polichinelle' was broken, though happily no one guessed it, and hitherto it had been enough to show them the box.

CHAPTER XIII—CHRYSEIS AND BRISEIS

'The child
Restore, I pray, her proffered ransom take,
And in His priest, the Lord of Light revere.
    Then through the ranks assenting murmurs rang,
The priest to reverence, and the ransom take.'

HOMER (DERBY).

For one moment, before emerging from the forest, looking through an opening in the trees, down a steep slope, a group of children could be seen on the grass in front of the huts composing the adowara, little brown figures in scanty garments, lying about evidently listening intently to the figure, the gleam of whose blonde hair showed her instantly to be Estelle de Bourke.

However, either the deputation had been descried, or Eyoub may have made some signal, for when the calvalcade had wound about through the remaining trees, and arrived among the huts, no one was to be seen. There was only the irregular square of huts built of rough stones and thatched with reeds, with big stones to keep the thatch on in the storm; a few goats were tethered near, and there was a rush of the great savage dogs, but they recognised Eyoub and Lanty, and were presently quieted.

'This is the chief danger,' whispered Lanty.

'Pray heaven the rogues do not murder them rather than give them up!'

The Sunakite, beginning to make strange contortions and mutterings in a low voice, seemed to terrify Eyoub greatly. Whether he pointed it out or not, or whether Eyoub was induced by his gestures to show it, was not clear to Arthur's mind; but at the chief abode, an assemblage of two stone hovels and rudely-built walls, the party halted, and made a loud knocking at the door, Hadji Eseb's solemn tones bidding those within to open in the name of Allah.

It was done, disclosing a vista of men with drawn scimitars. The Marabout demanded without ceremony where were the prisoners.

'At yonder house,' he was answered by Yakoub himself, pointing to the farther end of the village.

'Dog of a liar,' burst forth the Sunakite. 'Dost thou think to blind the eyes of the beloved of Allah, who knoweth the secrets of heaven and earth, and hath the sigil of Suleiman Ben Daoud, wherewith to penetrate the secret places of the false?'

The ferocious-looking guardians looked at each other as though under the influence of supernatural terror, and then Hadji Eseb spoke: 'Salaam Aleikum, my children; no man need fear who listens to the will of Allah, and honours his messengers.'

All made way for the dignified old man and his suite, and they advanced into the court, where two men with drawn swords were keeping guard over the captives, who were on their knees in a corner of the court.

The sabres were sheathed, and there was a shuffling away at the advance of the Marabouts, Sheyk Yakoub making some apology about having delayed to admit such guests, but excusing himself on the score of supposing they were emissaries sent by those whose authority he so defied that he had sworn to slaughter his prisoners rather than surrender them.

Hadji Eseb replied with a quotation from the Koran forbidding cruelty to the helpless, and sternly denounced wrath on the transgressors, bidding Yakoub draw off his savage bodyguard.

The man was plainly alarmed, more especially as the Sunakite broke out into one of his wild wails of denunciation, waving his hands like a prophet of wrath, and predicting famine, disease, pestilence, to these slack observers of the law of Mohammed.

This completed the alarm. The bodyguard fled away pell-mell, Yakoub after them. His women shut themselves into some innermost recesses, and the field was left to the Marabouts and the prisoners, who, not understanding what all this meant, were still kneeling in their corner. Hadji Eseb bade Arthur and the interpreter go to reassure them.

At their advance a miserable embrowned figure, barefooted and half clad in a ragged haik, roped round his waist, threw himself before the fair-haired child, crying out in imperfect Arabic, 'Spare her, spare her, great Lord! much is to be won by saving her.'

'We are come to save her,' said Arthur in French. 'Maître Hébert, do you not know me?'

Hubert looked up. 'M. Arture! M. Arture! Risen from the dead!' he cried, threw himself into the young man's arms, and burst out into a vehement sob; but in a second he recovered his manners and fell back, while Estelle looked up.

'M. Arture,' she repeated. 'Ah! is it you? Then, is my mamma alive and safe?'

'Alas! no,' replied Arthur; 'but your little brother is safe and well at Algiers, and this good man, the Marabout, is come to deliver you.'

'My mamma said you would protect us, and I knew you would come, like Mentor, to save us,' said Estelle, clasping her hands with ineffable joy. 'Oh, Monsieur! I thank you next to the good God and the saints!' and she began fervently kissing Arthur's hand. He turned to salute the Abbé, but was shocked to see how much more vacant the poor gentleman's stare had become, and how little he seemed to comprehend.

'Ah!' said Estelle, with her pretty, tender, motherly air, 'my poor uncle has never seemed to understand since that dreadful day when they dragged him and Maître Hébert out into the wood and were going to kill them. And he has fever every night. But, oh, M. Arture, did you say my brother was safe?' she repeated, as if not able to dwell enough upon the glad tidings.

'And I hope you will soon be with him,' said Arthur. 'But, Mademoiselle, let me present you to the Grand Marabout, a sort of Moslem Abbé, who has come all this way to obtain your release.'

He led Estelle forward, when she made a courtesy fit for her grandmother's *salon*, and in very fluent Cabeleyze dialect gave thanks for the kindness of coming to release her, and begged him to excuse her uncle, who was sick, and, as you say here, 'stricken of Allah.'

The little French demoiselle's grace and politeness were by no means lost on the Marabout, who replied to her graciously; and at the sight of her reading M. Dessault's letter, which the interpreter presented to her, one of the suite could not help exclaiming, 'Ah! if women such as this will be went abroad in our streets, there would be nothing to hope for in Paradise.'

Estelle did not seem to have suffered in health; indeed, in Arthur's eyes, she seemed in these six weeks to have grown, and to have more colour, while her expression had become less childish, deeper, and higher. Her hair did not look neglected, though her dress—the same dark blue which she had worn on the voyage—had become very ragged and soiled, and her shoes were broken, and tied on with strips of rag.

She gave a little scream of joy when the parcel of clothes sent by the French Consul was given to her, only longing to send some to Victorine before she retired to enjoy the comfort of clean and respectable clothes; and in the meantime something was attempted for the comfort of her companions, though it would not have been safe to put them into Frankish garments, and none had been brought. Poor Hébert was the very ghost of the stout and important *maître d'hôtel*, and, indeed, the faithful man had borne the brunt of all the privations and sufferings, doing his utmost to shield and protect his little mistress and her helpless uncle.

When Estelle reappeared, dressed once more like a little French lady (at least in the eyes of those who were not particular about fit), she found a little feast being prepared for her out of the provisions sent by the consuls; but she could not sit down to it till Arthur, escorted by several of the Marabout's suite, had carried a share both of the food and the garments to Lanty and Victorine.

They, however, were not to be found. The whole adowara seemed to be deserted except by a few frightened women and children, and Victorine and her Irish swain had no doubt been driven off into the woods by Eyoub—no Achilles certainly, but equally unwilling with the great Pelides to resign Briseis as a substitute for Chryseis.

It was too late to attempt anything more that night; indeed, at sundown it became very cold. A fire was lighted in the larger room, in the centre, where there was a hole for the exit of the smoke.

The Marabouts seemed to be praying or reciting the Koran on one side of it, for there was a continuous chant or hum going on there; but they seemed to have no objection to the Christians sitting together on the other side conversing and exchanging accounts of their adventures. Maître Hébert could not sufficiently dilate on the spirit, cheerfulness, and patience that Mademoiselle had displayed through all. He only had to lament her imprudence in trying to talk of the Christian faith to the children, telling them stories of the saints, and doing what, if all the tribe had not been so ignorant, would have brought destruction on them all. 'I would not have Monseigneur there know of it for worlds,' said he, glancing at the Grand Marabout.

'Selim loves to hear such things,' said Estelle composedly. 'I have taught him to say the Paternoster, and the meaning of it, and Zuleika can nearly say them.'

'*Miséricorde!*' cried M. Hubert. 'What may not the child have brought on herself!'

'Selim will be a chief,' returned Estelle. 'He will make his people do as he pleases, or he would do so; but now there will be no one to tell him about the true God and the blessed Saviour,' she added sadly.

'Mademoiselle!' cried Hébert in indignant anger—'Mademoiselle would not be ungrateful for our safety from these horrors.'

'Oh no!' exclaimed the child. 'I am very happy to return to my poor papa, and my brothers, and my grandmamma. But I am sorry for Selim! Perhaps some good mission fathers would go out to them like those we heard of in Arcadia; and by and by, when I am grown up, I can come back with some sisters to teach the women to wash their children and not scold and fight.'

The *maître d'hôtel* sighed, and was relieved when Estelle retired to the deserted women's apartments for the night. He seemed to think her dangerous language might be understood and reported.

The next morning the Marabout sent messengers, who brought back Yakoub and his people, and before many hours a sort of council was convened in the court of Yakoub's house, consisting of all the neighbouring heads of families, brown men, whose eyes gleamed fiercely out from under their haiks, and who were armed to the teeth with sabres, daggers, and, if possible, pistols and blunderbusses of all the worn-out patterns in Europe—some no doubt as old as the Thirty Years War; while those who could not attain to these weapons had the long spears of their ancestors, and were no bad representatives of the Amalekites of old.

After all had solemnly taken their seats there was a fresh arrival of Sheyk Abderrahman and his ferocious-looking following. He himself was a man of fine bearing, with a great black beard, and a gold-embroidered sash stuck full of pistols and knives, and with poor Madame de Bourke's best pearl necklace round his neck. His son Selim was with him, a slim youth, with beautiful soft eyes glancing out from under a haik, striped with many colours, such as may have been the coat that marked Joseph as the heir.

There were many salaams and formalities, and then the chief Marabout made a speech, explaining the purpose of his coming, diplomatically allowing that the Cabeleyzes were not subject to the Dey of Algiers, but showing that they enjoyed the advantages of the treaty with France, and that therefore they were bound to release the unfortunate shipwrecked captives, whom they had already plundered of all their property. So far Estelle and Arthur, who were anxiously watching, crouching behind the wall of the deserted house court, could follow. Then arose yells and shouts of denial, and words too rapid to be followed. In a lull, Hadji Eseb might be heard proffering ransom, while the cries and shrieks so well known to accompany bargaining broke out.

Ibrahim Aga, who stood by the wall, here told them that Yakoub and Eyoub seemed not unwilling to consent to the redemption of the male captives, but that they claimed both the females. Hébert clenched his teeth, and bade Ibrahim interfere and declare that he would never be set free without his little lady.

Here, however, the tumult lulled a little, and Abderrahman's voice was heard declaring that he claimed the Daughter of the Silkworm as a wife for his son.

Ibrahim then sprang to the Marabout's side, and was heard representing that the young lady was of high and noble blood. To which Abderrahman replied with the dignity of an old lion, that were she the daughter of the King of the Franks himself, she would only be a fit mate for the son of the King of the Mountains. A fresh roar of jangling and disputing began, during which Estelle whispered, 'Poor Selim, I know he would believe—he half does already. It would be like Clotilda.'

'And then he would be cruelly murdered, and you too,' returned Arthur.

'We should be martyrs,' said Estelle, as she had so often said before; and as Hubert shuddered and cried, 'Do not speak of such things, Mademoiselle, just as there is hope,' she answered, 'Oh no! do not think I want to stay in this dreadful place—only if I should have to do so—I long to go to my brother and my poor papa. Then I can send some good fathers to convert them.'

'Ha!' cried Arthur; 'what now! They are at one another's throats!'

Yakoub and Eyoub with flashing sabres were actually flying at each other, but Marabouts were seizing them and holding them back, and the Sunakite's chant arose above all the uproar.

Ibrahim was able to explain that Yakoub insisted that if the mistress were appropriated by Abderrahman, the maid should be his compensation. Eyoub, who had been the foremost in the rescue from the wreck, was furious at the demand, and they were on the point of fighting when thus withheld; while the Sunakite was denouncing woes on the spoiler and the lover of Christians, which made the blood of the Cabeleyzes run cold. Their flocks would be diseased, storms from the mountains would overwhelm them, their children would die, their name and race be cut off, if infidel girls were permitted to bewitch them and turn them from the faith of the Prophet. He pointed to young Selim, and demanded whether he were not already spellbound by the silken daughter of the Giaour to join in her idolatry.

There were howls of rage, a leaping up, a drawing of swords, a demand that the unbelievers should die at once. It was a cry the captives knew only too well. Arthur grasped a pistol, and loosened his sword, but young Selim had thrown himself at the Marabout's feet, sobbing out entreaties that the maiden's life might be saved, and assurances that he was a staunch believer; while his father, scandalised at such an exhibition on behalf of any such chattel as a female, roughly snatched him from the ground, and insisted on his silence.

The Marabouts had, at their chief's signal, ranged themselves in front of the inner court, and the authority of the Hadji had imposed silence even on the fanatic. He spoke again, making them understand that Frankish vengeance in case of a massacre could reach them even in their mountains when backed by the Dey. And to Abderrahman he represented that the only safety for his son, the only peace for his tribe, was in the surrender of these two dangerous causes of altercation.

The 'King of the Mountains' was convinced by the scene that had just taken place of the inexpedience of retaining the prisoners alive. And some pieces of gold thrust into his hand by Ibrahim may have shown him that much might be lost by slaughtering them.

The Babel which next arose was of the amicable bargaining sort. And after another hour of suspense the interpreter came to announce that the mountaineers, out of their great respect, not for the Dey, but the Marabout, had agreed to accept 900 piastres as the ransom of all the five captives, and that the Marabout recommended an immediate start, lest anything should rouse the ferocity of the tribe again.

Estelle's warm heart would fain have taken leave of the few who had been kind to her; but this was impossible, for the women were in hiding, and she could only leave one or two kerchiefs sent from Algiers, hoping Zuleika might have one of them. Ibrahim insisted on her being veiled as closely as a Mohammedan woman as she passed out. One look between her and Selim might have been fatal to all; though hers may have been in all childish innocence, she did not know how the fiery youth was writhing in his father's indignant grasp, forcibly withheld from rushing after one who had been a new life and revelation to him.

Mayhap the passion was as fleeting as it was violent, but the Marabout knew it boded danger to the captives to whom he had pledged his honour. He sent them, mounted on mules, on in front, while he and his company remained in the rear, watching till Lanty and Victorine were driven up like cattle by Eyoub, to whom he paid an earnest of his special share of the ransom. He permitted no pause, not even for a greeting between Estelle and poor Victorine, nor to clothe the two unfortunates, more than by throwing a mantle to poor Victorine, who had nothing but a short petticoat and a scanty, ragged, filthy bournouse. She shrouded herself as well as she could when lifted on her mule, scarce perhaps yet aware what had happened to her, only that Lanty was near, muttering benedictions and thanksgivings as he vibrated between her mule and that of the Abbé.

It was only at the evening halt that, in a cave on the mountain-side, Estelle and Victorine could cling to each other in a close embrace with sobs of joy; and while Estelle eagerly produced clothes from her little store of gifts, the poor *femme de chambre* wept for joy to feel indeed that she was free, and shed a fresh shower of tears of joy at the sight of a brush and comb.

Lanty was purring over his foster-brother, and cosseting him like a cat over a newly-recovered kitten, resolved not to see how much shaken the poor Abbé's intellect had been, and quite sure that the reverend father would be altogether himself when he only had his *soutane* again.

CHAPTER XIV—WELCOME

'Well hath the Prophet-chief your bidding done.'

Moore (LallaRookh).

Bugia was thoroughly Moorish, and subject to attacks of fanaticism. Perhaps the Grand Marabout did not wholly trust the Sunakite not to stir up the populace, for he would not take the recovered captives to his palace, avoided the city as much as possible, and took them down to the harbour, where, beside the old Roman quay, he caused his trusty attendant, Reverdi, to hire a boat to take them out to the French tartane—Reverdi himself going with them to ensure the fidelity of the boatmen. Estelle would have kissed the good old man's hand in fervent thanks, but, child as she was, he shrank from her touch as an unholy thing; and it was enforced on her and Victorine that they were by no means to remove their heavy mufflings till they were safe on board the tartane, and even out of harbour. The Frenchman in command of the vessel was evidently of the same mind, and, though enchanted to receive them, sent them at once below. He said his men had been in danger of being mobbed in the streets, and that there were reports abroad that the harem of a great Frank chief, and all his treasure, were being recovered from the Cabeleyzes, so that he doubted whether all the influence of the Grand Marabout might prevent their being pursued by corsairs.

Right glad was he to recognise the pennant of the *Calypso* outside the harbour, and he instantly ran up a signal flag to intimate success. A boat was immediately put off from the frigate, containing not only Lieutenant Bullock, but an officer in scarlet, who had no sooner come on deck than he shook Arthur eagerly by the hand, exclaiming,

''Tis you, then! I cannot be mistaken in poor Davie's son, though you were a mere bit bairn when I saw you last!'

'Archie Hope!' exclaimed Arthur, joyfully. 'Can you tell me anything of my mother?'

'She was well when last I heard of her, only sore vexed that you should be cut off from her by your own fule deed, my lad! Ye've thought better of it now?'

Major Hope was here interrupted by the lieutenant, who brought an invitation from Captain Beresford to the whole French party to bestow themselves on board the *Calypso*. After ascertaining that the Marabout had taken up their cause, and that the journey up Mount Couco and back again could not occupy less than twelve or fourteen days, he had sailed for Minorca, where he had obtained sanction to convey any of the captives who might be rescued to Algiers. He had also seen Major Hope, who, on hearing of the adventures of his young kinsman, asked leave of absence to come in search of him, and became the guest of the officers of the *Calypso*.

Arthur found himself virtually the head of the party, and, after consultation with Ibrahim Aga and Maître Hébert, it was agreed that there would be far more safety, as well as better accommodation, in the British ship than in the French tartane, and Arthur went down to communicate the proposal to Estelle, whom the close, little, evil-smelling cabin was already making much paler than all her privations had done.

'An English ship,' she said. 'Would my papa approve?' and her little prim diplomatic air sat comically on her.

'Oh yes,' said Arthur. 'He himself asked the captain to seek for you, Mademoiselle. There is peace between our countries, you know.'

'That is good,' she said, jumping up. 'For oh! this cabin is worse than it is inside Yakoub's hut! Oh take me on deck before I am ill!'

She was able to be her own little charming French and Irish self when Arthur led her on deck; and her gracious thanks and pretty courtesy made them agree that it would have been ten thousand pities if such a creature could not have been redeemed from the savage Arabs.

The whole six were speedily on board the *Calypso*, where Captain Beresford received the little heroine with politeness worthy of her own manners. He had given up his own cabin for her and Victorine, purchased at Port Mahon all he thought she could need, and had even recollected to procure clerical garments for the Abbé—a sight which rejoiced Lanty's faithful heart, though the poor Abbé was too ill all the time of the voyage to leave his berth. Arthur's arrival was greeted by the Abyssinian with an inarticulate howl of delight, as the poor fellow crawled to his feet, and began kissing them before he could prevent it. Fareek had been the pet of the sailors, and well taken care of by the boatswain. He was handy, quick, and useful, and Captain Bullock thought he might pick up a living as an attendant in the galley; but he showed that he held himself to belong absolutely to Arthur, and rendered every service to him that he could, picking up what was needful in the care of European clothes by imitation of the captain's servant, and showing a dexterity that made it probable that his cleverness had been the cause of the loss of a tongue that might have betrayed too much. To young Hope he seemed like a sacred legacy from poor Tam, and a perplexing one, such as he could hardly leave in his dumbness to take the chances of life among sailors.

His own plans were likewise to be considered, and Major Hope concerned himself much about them. He was a second cousin—a near relation in Scottish estimation—and no distant neighbour. His family were Tories, though content to submit to the House of Hanover, and had always been on friendly terms with Lady Hope.

'I writ at once, on hearing of you, to let her know you were in safety,' said the major. 'And what do you intend the noo?'

'Can I win home?' anxiously asked Arthur. 'You know I never was attainted!'

'And what would ye do if you were at home?'

'I should see my mother.'

'Small doubt of the welcome she would have for you, my poor laddie,' said the major; 'but what next?' And as Arthur hesitated, 'I misdoubt greatly whether Burnside would give you a helping hand if you came fresh from colloguing with French Jacobites, though my father and all the rest of us at the Lynn aye told him that he might thank himself and his dour old dominie for your prank—you were but a schoolboy then—you are a man now; and though your poor mother would be blithe to set eyes on you, she would be sairly perplexed what gate you had best turn thereafter. Now, see here! There's talk of our being sent to dislodge the Spaniards from Sicily. You are a likely lad, and the colonel would take my word for you if you came back with me to Port Mahon as a volunteer; and once under King George's colours, there would be pressure enough from all of us Hopes upon Burnside to gar him get you a commission, unless you win one for yourself. Then you could gang hame when the time was served, a credit and an honour to all!'

'I had rather win my own way than be beholden to Burnside,' said Arthur, his face lighting at the proposal.

'Hout, man! That will be as the chances of war may turn out. As to your kit, we'll see to that! Never fear. Your mother will make it up.'

'Thanks, Archie, with all my heart, but I am not so destitute,' and he mentioned Yusuf's legacy, which the major held that he was perfectly justified in appropriating; and in answer to his next question, assured him that he would be able to retain Fareek as his servant.

This was enough for Arthur, who knew that the relief to his mother's mind of his safety and acceptance as a subject would outweigh any disappointment at not seeing his face, when he would only be an unforgiven exile, liable to be informed against by any malicious neighbour.

He borrowed materials, and had written a long letter to her before the *Calypso* put in at Algiers. The little swift tartane had forestalled her; and every one was on the watch, when Estelle, who had been treated like a little princess on board, was brought in the long-boat with all her party to the quay. Though it was at daybreak, not only the European inhabitants, but Turks, Arabs, Moors, and Jews thronged the wharf in welcome; and there were jubilant cries as all the five captives could be seen seated in the boat in the light of the rising sun.

M. Dessault, with Ulysse in his hand, stood foremost on the quay, and the two children were instantly in each other's embrace. Their uncle had to be helped out. He was more bewildered than gratified by the welcome. He required to be assured that the multitudes assembled meant him no harm, and would not move without Lanty; and though he bowed low in return to M. Dessault's greeting, it was like an automaton, and with no recognition.

Estelle, between her brother and her friend, and followed by all the rest, was conducted by the French Consul to the chapel, arranged in one of the Moorish rooms. There stood beside the altar his two chaplains, and at once mass was commenced, while all threw themselves on their knees in thankfulness; and at the well-known sound a ray of intelligence and joy began to brighten even poor Phelim's features.

Arthur, in overflowing joy, could not but kneel with the others; and when the service concluded with the Te Deum's lofty praise, his tears dropped for joy and gratitude that the captivity was over, the children safe, and himself no longer an outcast and exile.

He had, however, to take leave of the children sooner than he wished, for the *Calypso* had to sail the next day.

Ulysse wept bitterly, clung to him, and persisted that he *was* their secretary, and must go with them. Estelle, too, had tears in her eyes; but she said, half in earnest, 'You know, Mentor vanished when Télémaque came home! Some day, Monsieur, you will come to see us at Paris, and we shall know how to show our gratitude!'

Both Lanty and Maître Hébert promised to write to M. Arture; and in due time he received not only their letters but fervent acknowledgments from the Comte de Bourke, who knew that to him was owing the life and liberty of the children.

From Lanty Arthur further heard that the poor Abbé had languished and died soon after reaching home. His faithful foster-brother was deeply distressed, though the family had rewarded the fidelity of the servants by promoting

Hébert to be intendant of the Provençal estates, while Lanty was wedded to Victorine, with a *dot* that enabled them to start a flourishing *perruquier's* shop, and make a home for his mother when little Jacques outgrew her care.

Estelle was in due time married to a French nobleman, and in after years 'General Sir Arthur Hope' took his son and daughter to pay her a long visit in her Provençal *château*, and to converse on the strange adventures that seemed like a dream. He found her a noble lady, well fulfilling the promise of her heroic girlhood, and still lamenting the impossibility of sending any mission to open the eyes of the half-converted Selim.